Ambrose Clarke, James H. Graff

The Story of a Honeymoon

Ambrose Clarke, James H. Graff

The Story of a Honeymoon

ISBN/EAN: 9783743324367

Manufactured in Europe, USA, Canada, Australia, Japa

Cover: Foto ©Andreas Hilbeck / pixelio.de

Manufactured and distributed by brebook publishing software
(www.brebook.com)

Ambrose Clarke, James H. Graff

The Story of a Honeymoon

THE

STORY OF A HONEYMOON

BY

CHAS. H. ROSS AND AMBROSE CLARKE

WITH NUMEROUS ILLUSTRATIONS

London:

WARD, LOCK, AND TYLER,

WARWICK HOUSE, PATERNOSTER ROW.

THE

STORY OF A HONEYMOON.

CHAPTER I.

WE MAKE A BAD BEGINNING AND COME IN FOR
A CURLY-TAILED DOG.

I *AM* married!

Please to italicize the "am," and put, if possible, a triumphant curl into the note of admiration.

Yes, I am married. The affair made some little
stir, I have reason to believe, out HOXTON way, and
was mentioned at more than one tea-table in TUF-
NELL Park. It has been, I will allow, some time in
coming off; but it has come off now—very much
so, indeed, and I AM MARRIED!

There was a breakfast, of course, and a blessing.
Also a slipper (which hit me); but it was thought
advisable to dispense with the tour.

We therefore begin life right off in HIGHLOW
Terrace, and our friends see us in.

She also mentions, while upon the subject, that the cellar's mouldy, and the kitchen fire won't burn. Furthermore, she wishes to know whether she can have a holiday the day after to-morrow.

I see the dew-drops on my ROSE—which is my poetical expression (registered) for tears in my wife's eyes. I comfort her. She shivers.

In the morning I send for MR. COMPO, my landlord.

He is a red-faced man, with a two-foot rule for ever sticking from his pocket. His manner is un-courteous, his style abrupt, his boots muddy.

" Well," says he, planting the dirty boots on my new carpet, " what's up, sir ?"

I say, " The wash-house is flooded."

" Ah !" he answers, " it will dry up right enough when the fine weather comes."

Says my wife, " Yes ; but there's a hole in the roof, and the rain comes in ; and you must mend it, MR. COMPO."

" Ah !" he says, " that's strange in a new house."

I say, " It is—very."

He says, " You'd better have it looked to with-out loss of time."

But I suggest, " Why not you ?"

" Show me the 'greement," he replies. " Let me see it in writing that I got to do it, and then I'll set about it."

I know, and he knows, there is no agreement. My wife and I look blankly at each other. MR. COMPO whistles.

After a while, MR. COMPO says he doesn't wish to be hard upon me.

I feel grateful.

He says he thinks he sees his way. I am more grateful. His way that he sees is that I should give him five pounds and leave it all to him. He refuses to have it all left to him without the money, so I give him two pound ten, and he goes away. In the course of the afternoon he sends two lads and a ladder. The ladder is laid on a flower-bed sown with the choicest seed. The lads seat themselves on my door-step and play at shove-half-penny.

The day passes by. In the evening MR. COMPO comes again, redder in the face, particularly about the nose—muddier in the person, particularly about the boots. He wants to see me. He has his wish. His speech is thick—his utterance is indistinct. He expresses his desire to "fetch some one a sender," which I do not encourage. He expresses a further desire to drink, adding, at my expense, which I refuse to entertain. He expresses an opinion that I am no gentleman, and then calls upon me for a song. I retreat. He howls defiance after me.

He continues to howl. A policeman appears. I tell him to turn MR. COMPO out of the house. He says he has no authority. Eventually MR. COMPO falls out himself. I close the door. Quiet reigns, and I am happy

In an hour's time I hear noises in the kitchen, and find the policeman making himself at home. In answer to my question, he says he's been looking at the window-fastenings.

I ask him the name of his inspector, and he says, "Walker."

Servant laughs. I wonder why. Policeman adds, furthermore, it's dry work looking at window-fastenings, and he'd like to drink my health, if it's all the same to me.

It isn't all the same to me; but he departs with the avowed intention of drinking my health, touching his hat, till I begin to think there's something wrong. Looking in my purse, I find I've given him half-a-sovereign instead of sixpence.

Later on I hear a giggling in the kitchen. Go down and find the servant cleaning a pair of boots. Ask her if she's been giggling? She says, "Lor', no;" and hazards a guess that it might have been the black beetles. ROSE ANNA doesn't think it likely.

Midnight—Bed. Sleep? No. Noises, whisperings, and *hammerings outside the window.*

It isn't beetles this time. ROSE ANNA trembles, and suggests thieves. She also hints at murder. Where are my pistols?

If I have any pistols in the house, of which I am very doubtful, they must be at the bottom of an unpacked box; the swordstick has not been seen; ROSE ANNA trembles, and the whisperings continue!

ROSE ANNA wants to know why I don't do something. Ha! ha! A bright idea—the poker!

I seize the poker, draw the blinds aside, and open the window. What do I see? Nothing. Yes. Wait a moment. There is the ladder reared up close to the window, and somebody is mounting it, I am bound to add, unsteadily, as he appears to miss every other step. A head rises gradually, a head without a hat, and, as far as I can discover from my position, without a body.

It rises till it reaches my level, when it hiccoughs and begs my pardon. I recognize in the voice that of my landlord, MR. COMPO. He says (all in one word) "Iopeidon'tintrude."

I ask him, with dignity, to explain himself. He laughs. I tell him AN ENGLISHMAN'S HOUSE IS HIS CASTLE! He says, "Is it?" and seems much impressed.

ROSE ANNA, in a muffled voice, partly fright and partly blankets, says, "Send him away." I point out to him that he had better descend. He doesn't appear to see it, but insists that I'm "joll'-goo'-f'ler," and that he wants to "pollygize." I say, "In the morning," adding, "get out," as he lays his hand on the window-sill. He doesn't move, so I push him gently.

Horror! He disappears with startling rapidity, and I hear an awful crash amongst the flower-pots below!

What have I done? I listen. All is silent.

Presently, I hear groans and a rattling amongst the flower-pots. I wait, breathless. Presently, there is a sound of snoring. He is snoring. Let him.

I go to bed again. I actually sleep. I dream I am in a shipwreck. That the clouds thunder, that the ship strikes and bumps upon the rocks, that the captain cries, in a decidedly feminine voice, "For goodness' sake, *do* wake up," and then I open my eyes.

Some one is hammering at the street-door fit to break it in—thunder! Rose Anna is striking and shaking me—bumping on the rocks!

"What's the matter?" I ask, rubbing my eyes. Rose Anna explains she is sure the house is on fire. I listen, and fancy I hear my landlord's voice. I take a jug of water, I open the window softly, I discharge the contents of the jug over the figure standing at the door with the knocker in his hand. Horror! No sooner have I done so than a distant gas-light gleams upon his buttons, and I see it is a policeman.

He wants to know what I mean by it.

Terrible thought! He has found the dead or dying body of COMPO amongst the flower-pots. He has come to arrest me. I have not only committed murder, but *have assaulted the police in the execution of their duty!*

He wants to know, a second time, what I mean by it. I beg his pardon. ROSE ANNA suggests telling him I thought he was cats. He says I've spoilt his uniform. I tell him I'm very sorry. He coughs, and says I've given him cold. He further hints that all the public-houses are shut, and that a glass of brandy-and-water is the only thing to save him from rheumatic fever.

ROSE ANNA says, "Give him some hot brandy-and-water." There is no fire, and no hot water, I explain, and ask if neat brandy will do. He thinks it will ; at all events he will try. He does try.

He tries a second time. Then he explains he saw the ladder against the house, and knocked to know whether there were thieves inside. I convince him there are not. He goes away. Bed once more. Sleep.

* * * * * *

Morning.   I am up with the lark ; also with the dawn.   I sneeze.

Trembling, I look for the corpse of COMPO.   I find smashed flower-pots, trodden-down flower-beds, a broken tobacco-pipe ; but no corpse.

A cart stops at my door.   A hamper, a packing-case, and a carpet-bag are put at my feet, and a demand made for money, which I pay, neglecting a hint that driving a cart is dry work.

The packing case is directed in the spiky hand-writing of my wife's aunt, as is the hamper, also the carpet-bag.   ROSE ANNA has expectations in that quarter: the aunt is wealthy.   I open the packing-case, and find it to contain a wedding present—a china jar, very ugly and very much cracked.

I tug the other hamper.   Something inside moans.   I come over faint as I think of COMPO. Could he have packed up his own mangled body and sent it to his murderer ?   But that's nonsense. However, will it be safe to undo the lid ?

I put it to ROSE ANNA.   Has she a suggestion to make ?   She suggests babies.

The question is—if it is a baby, and we let it remain thus, shall we not have to answer for its suffocation ?   Let us ask the servant.

Meanwhile there are more moans from the interior, also a melancholy whine, and then—a bark !

Ha, ha! I see it all now, and pretend I knew it all along. Afterwards I hear the servant say to ROSE ANNA, "How pale master looked!" I must take an early opportunity of doing something courageous before that girl, or she will have a low opinion of my personal courage.

When the hamper is opened, we find a dog. I am not strong in dogs, and am rather doubtful of the breed, but it is a curly-tailed dog—very curly tailed; something like a watch-spring. I try to uncurl it. It curls up again in a moment. I try again—the dog bites me.

There is a note inside the hamper—" Enclosed dog, CARLO. Take care of him for my sake."

Bother her sake. However, ROSE ANNA objects to this suggestion. Her aunt has always been very kind to her. What has that to do with it? I maintain she is a stupid old woman. ROSE ANNA cries. It seems to me she is always crying. The servant looks on with a nasty grin. I hate servants with nasty grins. She evidently thinks I'm a brute. Subsequently I hear she says so. I hear her mention it over the wall to the girl next door.

But about the dog. ROSE ANNA thinks he must be hungry. I should say he is—rather. She feeds him. He has about twice as much as I could eat myself. He is still hungry.

ROSE ANNA says she can see he will be a capital house-dog, he barks so. Later on he pins the butcher's boy ; he also fastens upon the young gentleman from the greengrocer's. He breaks loose and chivies some other boys in the lane. From the way he licks his lips when he comes back again, I expect he must have had a bit out of one of them.

The rest of the day is taken up in watching him eat, watching him while he is asleep, and seeing him wake up again. I think, after all, I can be fond of him, if he would not bark so much. When supper-time comes the man has not sent the beer. The road is rather lonely, and the girl does not like going for it. I don't like it either, but I go. I take a jug.

CARLO is waiting for me when I come back. He is a good house-dog. He mistakes me for a thief, and won't let me come in. I call to him. He goes on mistaking me. I try to open the gate.

He has got me by the leg.

Somehow the beer-jug gets broken.

This is MR. COMPO, *our landlord, pursued by the faithful* CARLO *in the same manner as the faithful one pursued me—his master.*

THE CELEBRATED DOG, CARLO.

This represents my Rose Anna in the act of making the celebrated Carlo, aforesaid, sit up—and I never knew a dog sit up better till he fell down again.

CHAPTER II.

WE COME IN FOR ANOTHER WILD ANIMAL, AND
AUNT SOPHONISBA AND I HAVE A QUARREL IN
THE PASSAGE.

BY-THE-BYE, did I tell you I was a clerk in
COUTER and PHLIMSY'S Bank, and that I am
on extremely friendly terms with Mr. SIMPSON,
the head cashier ? If I have not told you, it is not
because I have forgotten it, for, to speak candidly,
my engagement there occupies so large a portion
of my existence, I have hardly time to think of
anything else. Indeed I scarcely understand, now,
how I found time to get married.

You may have noticed Mr. SIMPSON when you
have come to our place, and if so, have no doubt
observed that his head is very bald ; so when he
says to me one morning, "FULLALOVE, my boy,
I've got a little hare for you," I tell him I think he

wants it more than I do, and I wink at his polished cranium.

"No, no!" says he, blushing all over the bald part, "hare, you know—a furry beast—hare without an i."

"Good gracious!" I say—I'm a great fellow for my joke, as you may have noticed—"what can I do with a blind and furry beast? I'm not the keeper of a menagerie."

Upon this he bursts out laughing, and presently producing the noble quadruped, I take it home after hours, dangling it proudly, and am pleased to fancy the boys in the street take me for a noble sportsman.   When I reach HIGHLOW Terrace there is great excitement.   I fling my prize at ROSE ANNA'S feet and strike an attitude.   Unhappily, ROSE ANNA, who is inclined to be nervous, is frightened, and screams.

She wants to know whether it will bite.   Satisfied of its harmlessness, she smiles through her tears and timidly strokes it.   She calls it "a poor itty ting;" she also playfully asks me what is "my little game;" and I find out now that she looks upon it as a rabbit.   Upon my informing her of the truth, she says, "Are you sure?"

I regard the beast again, from a new point of view.   Am I sure?   I only go by what Mr. SIMPSON said; most likely he knew, unless he, also, went by hearsay. Under the circumstances, however, I feel I ought to know, and so stick to my previous statement, and say "undoubtedly" with decision.

The important question, however, is, what are we to do with the animal now we have got it? ROSE ANNA says, "Oh, hang it." I am surprised at this language, which sounds almost like an expletive, but presently a light dawns upon me; our servant MARIA is of the party, and she adds, "Draw it."

Thinking I see a chance for one of my jokes, I add, "Quarter it." MARIA looks at me angrily, as if I had insulted her. ROSE ANNA does not see the point either, and asks, "Why?" This is getting stupid, so I say, "Oh, I don't know—never mind."

MARIA is waiting to know how we will have the hare cooked. ROSE ANNA appeals to me, and I, with marvellous presence of mind, suggest, "In the usual way." She, however, says, "Which way?" I tell her we'll think it over.

If it had been a rabbit it might have been done a hundred different ways, as I have often read in an advertisement. I wish I had brought home the book at the same time as the hare. As it is, MARIA'S inquiries are rather a nuisance. Presently she is back again, wanting to know what she is to do with the fur. I fancy she is chaffing us, and say, "What do you mean ?—take it off." But ROSE ANNA spoils all by speaking of it as if it were trying to pass a Civil Service examination, and says, " Pluck it."

I am uneasy about this observation, thinking she cannot have used the right phrase ; and my suspicions are presently confirmed by hearing explosions of mirth in the passage. I wish we had never taken MARIA. She has a nasty jeering sort of way with her, to which I think I have already alluded ; but to set this matter straight I say, in ROSE ANNA'S defence, and in explanation to MARIA, " That is the French way."

MARIA replies, " It's a rum un ;" but does not enlighten us any further.

This is a half-holiday, of which I have had several lately. I have come home early to hang up pictures, and set to work at once with some large brass-headed nails. We are very careful in choosing the exact spot where the nail is to go in. Unfortunately, however, it won't go in there, because of a hard brick. When I try again, it goes in very easily, but won't hold fast, on account of the soft plaister. The provoking part of the business is, that I hang up a picture before I find this out, and so it falls down and the glass is broken.

Subsequently I knock in other nails up and down. ROSE ANNA also knocks in one or two.

On the whole the work, when finished, looks patchy. Later on I endeavour to fill the holes up with crumbs of bread, and afterwards try to think they cannot easily be noticed.

During this time MARIA goes on with the hare.

She has asked for some money for gravy-beef. I suppose it is all right, and give it her. She also wants port wine. I go to the chiffonier, and ask how much. She says she had better have a bottle, and I give her *the* bottle. She takes it, and the culinary operations are supposed to be progressing.

But time goes on. It grows dark. The dinner-hour arrives and passes by I begin to have a headache. ROSE ANNA is usually low-spirited about this period of the day, and thinks a good deal of her mother and the home she has left.

We think it best not to interfere with MARIA, and wait as patiently as we can. Presently I fancy I hear a giggling in the kitchen. I go down quickly, and find MARIA alone. The port-wine bottle is on the table, I pick it up and find that it is empty: but I can see or smell nothing of the hare.

MARIA looks confused and flushed. I suspect something wrong, and open the cellar-door. A militia-man comes out, like the man out of the weather-glass in wet weather. He salutes me in military fashion, and calls me " Captain !"

I feel that under the circumstances he ought to be kicked ; but there is a good deal of him. The question is, what can I do ? Suppose I ask him what he is doing there. I do so.

He can't tell me. He laughs. What am I to do now ?

I feel it is a moment when I must assert my-self, or henceforth, in the servant's eyes, I am no-where. The question is, where shall I be, on the other hand ? I risk all, and say, " Leave my house, sir."

The militia-man says, " All right, guv'nor," and moves towards the door.

This is most satisfactory. The expression of my eye has, then, quelled him. I look more fero-cious still, and say, " Immediately."

He says, " There's no hurry, guv'nor, is there ?"

This is not as satisfactory, and the servant seems inclined to giggle. I must assert myself again. I don't wish to excite him too much, but I must do something. I push him gently. He pushes me with less consideration, and I find my-self suddenly some yards off, leaning up against the wall. It is providential I did not take the direction of the cellar.

He says, "Don't try that on, guv'nor."

I ask, for the sake of saying something, "Are you going?" and he answers, as before, "There's no hurry, is there?" I think it best to make no reply, and wait with what dignity I can assume; and in due course he reaches the door and passes out. I follow him to the threshold, and when his back is turned, lunge out my leg with ferocity. I, however, think it best to avoid touching him, and the action gives me a crick in the knee. After this I immediately lock the door and bolt it.

He calls out something impertinent from the outside, and taps at the kitchen window; but I feel that further altercation would be unworthy of me, and with a withering glance at the girl, who is still giggling, I retire.

When I have closed the parlour door I tell ROSE ANNA that I kicked the fellow out. She says, "He might have hurt you."

I think it more than likely, but do not pursue the subject. Later on I hear the girl describing the scene to ROSE ANNA. She is giggling, and says, "Lor', how master did shake!"

One thing I am resolved upon. Either that woman or I quit the house to-morrow. As it is my house, perhaps it would not be unreasonable if she were the one to go.

*　　　*　　　*　　　*

Next morning we are at breakfast, and ROSE
ANNA turns suddenly pale. I ask in agitation
what is the matter. She says, " It's ant."

I reply, " What's ant ?" In reality I know what
she means, but I'm in one of my funny moods.
She answers again, in terms of cutting reproach,
that I ought to be ashamed of ridiculing the kind-
est old soul alive. I tell her a sole is a fish, and
an ant an insect, so that I cannot reconcile her two
statements. N.B.—This is some more of my fun ;
but she does not enter into it, rather sticking to
her original idea that I ought to be ashamed of
myself, and adding that I am a monster. I am
five feet two and a half. She also says she wishes
I wouldn't, and weeps.

I don't, and she recovers slowly. Then she
explains: Aunt SOPHY (short for SOPHONISBA)
has written to say she is coming to spend a day
with us. This ROSE ANNA had forgotten previously to mention. At hearing this, I say,
" Bother !" I wish we had been married a little
longer, that I might use stronger language. However, it's a relief to my feelings to go even so far.

While we are yet at breakfast, Aunt SOPHY
comes. Her name is BODKIN. She is fair and
fifty, and, as yet, unmarried. She retains the
bloom of youth—indeed, she buys it in packets at
the chemist's—she also adheres to the skittishness

of early maidenhood ; and she is under the impression that she has beautiful shoulders. Being,
if anything, over-plump, she is, when playful, inclined to be a little bouncy.

She says in her letter that she is coming to
spend a nice long day. She says she has been
pining to take ROSE ANNA to her heart. She is
usually pining to take some one in that direction.
She dates from a select boarding-house in a
favourite watering-place, and mentions, in a P.S.,
the number of "offers" she has had during the
previous month.

I say, "Stupid old woman !" ROSE ANNA
objects, pointing out that if she were old and
stupid she would not have so many offers ; on
which I amend my sentence, and say, "Stupid
young men."

Aunt SOPHY comes. ROSE ANNA says I had
better behave myself. I do. I wait at the end of
the road for her cab. She comes to the wrong end,
and I go on waiting ever so long for nothing.

Presently the servant fetches me. When I
arrive in the house, Aunt SOPHY bounces out of
the parlour and bounces on to my bosom. I don't
expect it, and give way awkwardly. The servant,
as usual, giggles.

After this, Aunt SOPHY bounces back into the
parlour. There is no room for bouncing in our

parlour, and she upsets a side-table with her crino-
line. While picking up the pieces, I tell her I hear
crinolines are going out. She says she never
thought she should have worn one, but now she
has tried she never means to leave it off. On this
I say, I know for a fact that crinolines have quite
gone out, and only common persons wear them.
She sniffs at me defiantly, and I see that she and I
won't be friends.

She goes on sniffing, and I suppose it is still at
me; but at last she says she smells the gas es-
caping somewhere. She has not been in the house
five minutes before she has found out it is damp.
After a time she settles the smell to her satisfaction,
and says, " Drains."

To amuse her, we propose a survey over the
house and grounds. We begin with the grounds, and
exhaust them prematurely. As for the house, she
finds it is tumbling down. The fastenings are discovered to be insecure, and the water-pipes leaky.
With regard to the rooms generally she says—poky.
With reference to the chimneys, one and all—
smoky. Pointing to AUNT SOPHY, I say in a
whisper to ROSE ANNA—croaky. This is another
of my jokes, and as successful as usual. Then we
have lunch.

She asks if we received the vase all right (her
present). We say, yes; but such a pity it is so

cracked. AUNT SOPHY screams. This is its beauty. I look at it with one of my quiet smiles. Ugly rubbish—the vase I mean, not the aunt—only fit to grow mustard-and-cress in.

AUNT SOPHY continues. "And dear CARLO, where is he?" Where, indeed? I have not seen the beast for some time. I go out and whistle. I hear a bark and cries in the garden. He is limbing some one as usual. It is COMPO. MR. COMPO is outside, twirling round and round, looking for his coat-tails. CARLO is savagely tearing and rending the said tails. I say, "CARLO, CARLO! Good dog!"

COMPO says, "What do you mean? don't set him at me."

I explain: when I say good dog I mean bad dog, and add that I wish the brute was dead and buried.

AUNT SOPHY overhears me, and is indignant. She says she is glad to know how her presents are valued. Meanwhile CARLO is still worrying COMPO's coat-tails. AUNT SOPHY tries to call him off. The dog flies at her instead, and makes a snap at her curls.

Horror! they come out by the root or off by the skin. COMPO laughs. ROSE ANNA laughs, and pretends it is at something else. I and AUNT SOPHY remain serious. AUNT SOPHY puts on her front again a good deal awry, and we go on talking, and we look more serious than ever. But, presently, it falls again, on to the top of her nose; and this time I can't stand it any longer, but go off with an explosion.

Then AUNT SOPHY fires up, and calls for her bonnet and shawl. We try to pacify her, but she won't be pacified, and leaves the house in a fury. I should feel rather pleased, only ROSE ANNA looks at the affair seriously, and bursts into tears again.

Bother ROSE ANNA's tears!

There was a breakfast of course, and a blessing.

TULLALOVE IN THE CHARACTER OF AN INJURED HUSBAND.

There is some awkwardness in broaching the business I have come about. However, I open matters thus—

"Hallo, you sir!" I say.

"Hallo!" he says.

[Rather a long pause occurs at this point.]

CHAPTER III.

LIFE is not altogether a bed of roses in HIGH-
LOW Terrace.

I won't say anything about the black beetles. I
will not allude to the grinning servant. No mention
shall be made of the flooded washhouse. Neither
shall there be any reference to the policeman ; nor
to the soldier ; nor to COMPO ; nor, if you come to
that, even to AUNT SOPHY. But, these little matters being treated as mere trifles, there are, still, the
neighbours ; and about them I have a word to say,
and now is the time to say it.

It is my opinion that the neighbours make fun
of me.

They lie in wait for me. They hide their faces
in their handkerchiefs when I pass, and explode
with laughter the moment after.

They double up at sight of me. If I were a comic actor, I shouldn't mind it. It is what happened, I have read, to LISTON, WRIGHT, and JOE GRIMALDI ; and I suppose they felt gratified—but I do not. It is not my line. I have never gone in for that sort of thing. I am in a bank, as I have said, and have a certain character to keep up ; and I'm pretty well certain COUTER and PHLIMSY would not like it.

But let them laugh! I don't care so much about that, after all. Let them laugh as long as they like ; but don't let them wink. If any of them are compelled, by habit or the air of HIGHLOW Terrace, to contract one eyelid occasionally, let it be the females who do so ; and, further, let it be when *I* am passing—not the males when ROSE ANNA approaches.

ROSE ANNA laughs, and says I'm jealous! Ha, ha!—jealous! Still I wish she didn't seem to like it so much when that conceited jackanape opposite strolls about, smoking his penny cigar in his twopenny-halfpenny garden. He is standing there now, like a dummy outside a cheap tailor's shop; only he's winking, as usual ; also smoking ; likewise making pantomimic signs, like the clown that he is. By the bye, where is ROSE ANNA?

I appeal to our servant—she has not gone yet, because we cannot get suited in a moment—and she says, "Missus is watering them jerryniams at the bedroom windy."

My blood boils; my manly bosom heaves with suppressed emotion.

"Ask your mistress to come to me," I say, in majestic tones. The servant grins as usual, but I pretend not to notice it.

Presently she comes back with a broader grin than ever, and says, "Missus is busy."

My blood goes on boiling, but I think it best not to enter into any argument. ROSE ANNA keeps on watering the plants; the DON JUAN opposite keeps on winking.

I scowl; he smiles. I shake my fist; he kisses his hand. The fact is, he does not see me, but is gazing with one eye through a glass at my ROSE ANNA watering the geraniums, while he winks at her with the other. How is this to end?

I think the matter over as calmly as possible. Suppose I have his blood? or shall I give him in charge? I wonder how much MR. MACE would want to thrash him for me. Stop! I have it. I will send him a politely sarcastic message by the servant. By the bye, did I tell you my forte lies in quiet sarcasm? I'm told it is a little too quiet sometimes; but when it goes home it stings.

The grinning baboon responds to my call. Does she see the person opposite? The which?

The person with the glass. He does seem as
stylish a gent, she says, as she would wish to set
eyes on. She also observes, that he is one of her
sort. I tell her I want to know nothing about her
sort, but desire her to take the person a message
from me.

The message is delivered : it is—" My respectful compliments, and would he wink at somebody
else's window ?"

She grins as I deliver it to her, and retires
grinning. I can't see her face as she crosses the
road ; but by the curve of her back, I feel certain
that she is still grinning as hard as ever. I hide
and watch, to see the winker wither at my cutting
words. Somehow he doesn't wither : he grins
also.

He says, loud enough for all the terrace to
hear,—" Why don't Mr. FULLALOVE bring his own
message ?"

I don't hear what she says ; but, by the expression of her back, I take it to be,—" Because he
daren't !" My blood is still boiling, but I rather
wish it was all over.

The woman's grin, as she returns, is diabolical.
The corners of her mouth seem to meet at the
back of her neck. She says the gentleman recom-
mends me to go to Bath.

This is becoming serious. I wish it were not

so; but I don't see how I can do less than have his blood, under the circumstances. Perhaps a cutting rejoinder might have some effect; but I can think of nothing at the moment. He might yet be withered with a word, if that word was handy; but it isn't.

No, there is nothing but his blood!—and how shall I have it? With a walking-stick.

I take a good-sized walking-stick, and cross the road. Arrived there, there is some awkwardness in broaching the business I have come about. However, I open matters thus:

" Hallo, you sir!" I say.

" Hallo!" he says.

Rather a long pause occurs at this point. Then he says,—" What do you want?"

I request that he won't wink. He says he shall if he likes. I say he shan't. He winks violently with both eyes for several moments, and laughs. I tell him not to let me see him do it again. He does it again instantly. I feel I am losing ground.

I could wither him even now, if I could only think of something withering. He wants to know if I have any more to say. I say that he is a disgrace to the terrace, and that he ought to be ashamed of himself.

I add that I have a great mind to chastise him

for his insolence.   He cowers, and implores me not to hurt him, for the sake of his widowed mother.

Bother his widowed mother! Why should I spare him on that account? I tell him he is no gentleman, and a profligate. I give him a word or two of sound advice, and caution him to take care what he is about for the future. I am getting on first-rate.

He is evidently moved, and presses his handkerchief to his eyes. I am turning away when I suddenly catch him kissing his hand to my windows. I raise the stick, and, somehow or other, the next moment it is whirling through the air, and I receive a violent blow on the chest, followed by another on the nose.

Undoubtedly this is the moment for action ; but what action? As far as I can analyze my feelings, I am inclined to cry. I am conscious of winking violently myself. My antagonist asks if I want any more. I can't say I do. I should like to give him something, though, but don't see my way clear.

In the distance I catch sight of MARIA, doubled up with laughter. I feel as if I should like to go home ; but I am conscious my dignity will suffer if I beat a retreat. I stand my ground, therefore, and observe my nose is rapidly swelling.

The winker meanwhile smiles, and lights a cigar. I demand an apology. He says he hasn't any on hand. I say I will summon him. He doesn't seem to care. I don't know what else to say, so subside into silence.

I begin to wonder whether ROSE ANNA has seen any of this, and how many heads are at the windows of the opposite houses. I look round, and find that I have got a large and appreciative audience. The winker says, " Go home to bed."

There is some reason in this, though it is rather insulting. I look round the side of my nose, and scowl upon him as much as I can under such disadvantageous circumstances, and stalk away slowly. Half way across the road I hear a noise behind me. I think it is his footstep, and jump a little. It was only a pebble he had thrown ; but the people at the windows all laugh.

In-doors I find ROSE ANNA in tears and terror. " What have you been doing ?" she asks. " Did he hit you very hard ?"

I don't like that way of putting it, and say, " The affair is not finished yet."

She says, " Oh ! pray leave him alone, dear. He will only hurt you."

I reply, " Will he ?" with ferocity. Secretly, I think it more than probable.

❋   ❋   ❋   ❋   ❋   ❋   ❋

Later on in the day I am soused in vinegar like
a mackerel, and wrapped in brown paper like a
parcel; but my blood is still boiling, and my intention is to be avenged.

ANNA MARIA *says, " What have you been doing ? Did he hit you very hard ?"*

THIS IS ROSE ANNA PICKING UP SOME OF OUR "BARGAINS."

I really do think, too, she looked very nice, but didn't the "bargains" turn out a pack of rubbish for all that.

CHAPTER IV.

DID I tell you we are rather weak in the way of
furniture?

Did I previously mention the fact that when
ROSE ANNA and I go from one room to the other,
we take our seats with us?

Didn't I? Well, I meant to.

It had always been my intention to furnish our
house with my little savings, and I had even entered into treaty with a well-known furnishing firm,
when an artful tempter whispered in my ear,
"Second-hand!" Hardly had his whisper died
away, when a fiend in human form suggested
"Sales;" and, leaving me doubting, brought back
with him a worse fiend than himself, who added
"Auction Marts," with an alluring smile. I was
tempted. I fell. The furniture is now arriving.

I see the van at the door. I see wooden legs
sticking out everywhere—furniture legs, I mean,
not the props of limbless Greenwich pensioners. It
is astonishing how cheap furniture shows up in legs.
It is still more astonishing how apt the said legs
are to separate from the articles they are intended
to support—usually with a report like a pistol.

I notice, besides legs, the top of my dining-
room table. I don't mind telling you, in a friendly
way, that the top is deal; but I do not see the
occasion for all HIGHLOW Terrace to be acquainted
with the fact that my polished mahogany legs only
support such a top. It is rather humiliating.

Of course there is a crowd of people at the
windows. I don't believe even the legs are mahogany.

The neighbours seem tremendously amused.
One old lady opposite has taken a chair, as though
it were a play. The finger of the terrace, so to
speak, is pointed at me when I go out on the steps
without my hat. I am overcome with confusion,
and run in again. Subsequently I appear in a
wide-awake.

There are a good lot of men come down with
the van. There is also an enormous quantity of
rope and no end of straw; some portions of the
latter hang about our front garden for a week or
two after.

I rather wish—though I don't exactly know why—that there were not so many chalk hieroglyphics upon my furniture. I also wish that the first things unpacked didn't happen to be one of my job lots—a knife-board, some flat irons, a bird-cage, a baby's chair, and all that sort of thing, which I really never intended to have had at all, only I was staring at the auctioneer in an absent moment, and he knocked them down to me, and I didn't like to have any bother about it.

The next article unloaded is a small looking-glass. I think it as well to look as if I were superintending something or other, and say, " Take care, please, will you ?" The man I address touches his hat and immediately lets fall the glass.

I say, " There !" He says, " Very sorry, sir." I think the matter over quietly before saying any more. Shall I be able to make the fellow pay for it ? I am doubtful on the point, and think it best to go no farther into the subject.

ROSE ANNA and the servant come out in front ; I wish they wouldn't. ROSE ANNA begins laughing. I don't think she ought to do so. What will the men think ? Besides, there are the neighbours.

ROSE ANNA wants to sit down on a recently unpacked chair. One of the men warns her off. He intimates that the said chair wasn't put together for sitting purposes. I ask, "Why?" He goes on to say, addressing ROSE ANNA, that the gov'nor (myself) had better try it first. I do so in all good faith, and find myself immediately afterwards sitting on the gravel path.

It is an attenuated chair, with mother-o'-pearl let into its back. I prided myself upon it when I made the purchase; now I grieve over its five fellows, equally attenuated and mother-o'-pearly, and doubtless, equally unstable. I threaten to send the set back.

The man says, confidentially, it won't be no manner o' good. Being pressed farther, he explains that they are part of a set of twelve chairs that have been already in four houses, and that one or more have been broken in each, and the lot sent back, till they were reduced to half a dozen, and that "the guv'nor" had said the next party who took them must keep them, or else it would go on till there wasn't a chair left.

Upon reflection, this seems a bad arrangement for me. I tell him so. He says, "It are," and whistles.

Observing this man with more attention than I have hitherto bestowed upon him, I conclude that he is the worse for liquor. Upon reflection, are not all the rest more or less in the same condition? I notice in their behaviour an awful recklessness.

As a rule, they let every other thing they unpack tumble. Those which escape this fate they bump against the passage wall or the door-post.

These misfortunes amuse the neighbours immensely. That brute of a girl of ours is on a perpetual broad grin; I inwardly pray that the wardrobe may fall on her.

As I wish this, the wardrobe does fall, but not on her. It falls on a wash-stand, and both go to pieces. One of the men says, " It must have been in the way it fell," and asks if I've got any glue.

I say indignantly, "Will you please to be more careful?" and, trying to carry a chair myself, I also tumble on my way up the steps. The neighbours are more amused than ever.

Taking refuge inside the house, I find ROSE ANNA crying among the ruins.

Before half the goods are brought in, it comes on to rain. I have my doubts about the things standing much water, and rush out again to help. I seize a maple-wood dressing-table and bear it in in triumph. It is only slightly wet. I wipe it with my pocket handkerchief. Horror! the grain comes off in streaks, disclosing very indifferent deal.

I am roused. I use bad language—to the table. ROSE ANNA sobs and wishes she were dead. That's not much assistance.

She looks as if she were about to faint. I fan
her with my handkerchief, forgetting its odours are
paint, varnish, and putty. It, however, revives her,
and she comes on my arm to the door to watch the
unloading. They are just now bringing in her
table—a pretty spindle-legged carved-and-twisted
article, of no use to any one. She is delighted
with it, though it is rather inclined to tip over when
touched.

The unloading is at an end, and the men want
beer. I previously mentioned that I was roused,
and am still in that condition. I therefore refuse
indignantly, and ask, what next? They are impudent, but finally retire.

We light a fire in the drawing-room to dry the
furniture, and go to dinner. At pudding we hear
a succession of cracks like pistol-shots. ROSE
ANNA says, " Fenians."

Of course I know what it is, though I don't say ;
and that grinning idiot of a servant, who is chang-
ing the plates, pretends to think I am frightened.

She says, " Lor', how pale master is! It's only
the new things splitting up."

We go into the drawing-room presently, and
find a dismal spectacle. Tables have warped, bits
of veneer have split off and lie curled up about the
room, and everything is sticky to the touch and
unpleasant to the smell.

ROSE ANNA sinks upon the sofa, which cracks alarmingly. She jumps up, and it cracks again, louder than before.

I say vaguely, "This sort of thing won't do." ROSE ANNA sobs out, "Oh, how could you? You ought to have known better." This is indeed cruel, but my heart is too full for utterance.

Chancing to look towards the door, I observe that CARLO has entered. He is smelling the new purchases, and picks up and eats a bit of the veneer lying on the floor. At this moment of bitter agony I have only one wish—

May it poison him!

*　　*　　⁂　　*　　❧

At last we are settled.

After many days of worry and annoyance, after bitter disappointments, cruel anxieties, and thrice blighted hopes—after, in fact, several little unpleasantries between ROSE ANNA and myself— we are settled in HIGHLOW Terrace.

We are happy; we are quiet; we are at liberty to enjoy ourselves; we mean to do so.

When I get home of an evening from COUTER and PHLIMSY'S (the hours are inconvenient for domestic arrangements, but I will not complain), ROSE ANNA twines her arms around my neck. She beseeches me, by my love and by my valour, to sit by her side as in the old times gone by, to smile as I was wont to smile, to talk as was my early custom, and, in the words of the poet, to " dally the hours away."

I do dally, and it is very delightful—if we didn't run short of subjects to talk about rather too quickly.

I have a faint remembrance of having helped to draw a mental picture, some months ago, in which ROSE ANNA and I played the parts of Shepherdess and Shepherd, *à la* WATTEAU, seated beneath an umbrageous shelter in our suburban garden. When we drew that picture, we forgot to put in the neighbours' windows, which are crowded like a family box at a pantomime if ever I venture outside the back door.

As to shade, the sweet-pea arbour has not grown as we expected.

When ROSE ANNA dreamt of a short white muslin skirt and a mossy bank, she never thought of green stains, and blacks flying from the chimneys round about us. Moreover, our genial summer climate is not altogether suited to such proceedings. Besides, as it is, ROSE ANNA has got a cold.

We neither of us now speak of fancy dress, nor is any allusion made to mossy banks ; nor indeed does the wife of my bosom quote poetry to me very often. On the contrary, she asks me to guess what she's got for dinner. I try to guess, and can't.

She says in a whisper, " Tripe," and laughs.

If there is one thing on which I dote it is tripe, but ROSE ANNA alone knows the secret. How could I, professing gentility, and living in HIGHLOW Terrace, confess my weakness publicly?

We sit down to dinner. MARIA (that woman is still with us, but under warning) brings in the tripe disdainfully, and slaps it down defiantly. A savour of onions fills the house to overflowing, but we are happy

ROSE ANNA'S cold is very bad. She ties a something of flannel round her head, and I give her a good stiff tumbler of grog after dinner. Her cold is so bad she cannot, she says, taste whether it is strong or weak. Her feet are on the fender, and her dress is folded across her lap.

She is about to sneeze. She has thrown up her fairy-like head, when a loud knock reverberates through the whole house, and arrests the sneeze in its progress. I have hardly time to say "good gracious," when MARIA, with one of her grins, throws open the parlour door and announces Mr. SMITH ; and my bachelor friend stalks in.

He is tall, and hits his head against the chande-lier in his eagerness to shake hands. He grasps

my fingers in a bony grip, and asks me, in a confidential and sympathizing whisper, how I find myself by this time, as if marriage were a dangerous
illness and he my doctor.

He is delighted and jubilant on hearing I am
well, but he is desponding and cast down on being
informed that ROSE ANNA has a cold. He sits
down by the fire, and puts his hat under his
chair.

After a pause, he says " Well ?"

I smile, and say " Well ?" like an echo.

ROSE ANNA, of course, wishes he had not
come, but, as he has come, wishes he would go
again. I observe that she glances nervously towards the sofa, round a corner of which the something of flannel is sticking out.

I tell SMITH, after a pause, that it was very
kind of him to come, and ask him if he will take
anything. He looks as if he would like to, but
ROSE ANNA quells him, and he says he won't.

This is lucky, as there are no spirits left, and it's
always a great risk whether MARIA won't be impudent if asked to go out at night on an errand.

I try to think of something to say to draw
SMITH out and make him take his eyes off the
something of flannel, which I catch him fixing. I
ask him what he's been doing lately ?

He says, "Oh, usual thing, you know.

Knocking about and enjoying life." Then he adds, " There's an end to all that for you, old fellow."

Rose Anna, I observe, is bridling.

He goes on to ask, who do I think he met last night ? " Why, Jack Spanker, who was with us the night when I would have that other bottle, and went afterwards—"

I beseech him, with an imploring glance, to change the conversation. He understands me. He winks. Rose Anna sees the wink, and evidently believes there is some frightful secret between us.

I have told her I was a terribly wild fellow once upon a time, which assertion has not the ghost of a foundation ; but most married men like to keep up a similar fiction.

Smith is an impostor also. He pretends to be fast, when he isn't. He goes on to say, " Well, old fellow, some time, when Mrs. Fullalove can spare you, we'll have a night of it, and go the old rounds."

What old rounds ? I haven't a notion. But Rose Anna can stand it no longer. Her eyes are wild as she declares vehemently, I have given up my old dissipations and dissolute companions.

Smith, taken aback, says he hopes not. Then, seeing his mistake, he declares he didn't mean that. Driven into a corner as to what he did mean, he stammers, and becomes confused, finally confessing he doesn't know what he means, and ROSE ANNA is left master of the field.

There is a dead silence after this, and SMITH thinks he had better go. Nobody says he hadn't ; so he gets up, and says, " Good-bye," backing on to his hat.

It occurs to me that we have behaved rather badly to SMITH. I ask him to come and spend a long day. I have a great mind to offer him a bed, but ROSE ANNA looks ferocious.

He hopes he has not intruded, and, on being told—in the expectation of his departure—" Not at all," he sits down again.

ROSE ANNA'S expression is appalling. She sits aloof, and we converse. The conversation languishes. I notice him glancing at the empty bottle, but I make no allusion to it. Finally, he gets up again and says he'll go, and really does go.

I let him out, and bolt the door after him with, I trust, not unseemly haste. ROSE ANNA says, " Thank goodness !" before he is well out of the passage.

Two minutes afterwards, I hear him in difficulties with CARLO in the garden. I hear him use bad language to the dog. I hear the dog use bad language to him. MARIA comes up and says CARLO'S pinned the gent against the water-butt. Hadn't I better go and help him ?

I doubt my power to be of much service, and say, doubtingly, " Perhaps I had."

ROSE ANNA says, perhaps I hadn't! She won't let me risk my valuable life in an encounter with wild beasts. Bless her dear little heart!

She adds, if I open the door, *that* SMITH will come back, and then there will be no getting rid of him. I hope ROSE ANNA'S affection for me is disinterested!

As to SMITH, he is still struggling. I hope he won't be hurt. I also hope he doesn't think we hear him. Presently CARLO is heard howling. SMITH has kicked him off. If he could only have killed him! but there's no such luck as that.

However, I'll get rid of that beast to-morrow, or I'll know the reason why!

CHAPTER V.

I SETTLE AFFAIRS WITH THE CURLY-TAILED DOG.

I WAKE in the morning with my vow of the preceding night still fresh in my memory. I will get rid of Carlo! I have sworn it!

But how?

I will not shed his blood, though he has mine on three separate occasions. I will not shed his blood, I repeat, for several reasons. The first is, I don't know exactly how I should manage it. Another is, that his appalling howls would disturb the neighbourhood. Another, that it would make. such a mess in our back garden.

I will drive him away; I will refuse him home and shelter, and let him wander a vagrant dog upon the earth till some brewer's dray or PICK-FORD'S van plays old JUGGERNAUT with him.

I go into the back garden with determination and a wide-awake on my manly brow. CARLO

FULLALOVE IN THE CHARACTER OF A MAN OF MYSTERY.

The party in the apron is the chemist, of whom I bought the poison. The other party, in the cap, is the boy who followed in my trail. I, FULLALOVE, will be observed in the far distance, only the distance is not as far off as it might have been.

He held him fast till the policeman relieved him of his charge.

thinks I'm his breakfast, and wags his tail. De-
luded beast! In course of time he finds out his
mistake, and growls. I endeavour to conciliate
him before commencing operations.

I say, "Good dog," and "Poor fellow," and pat
him with a hand which *will* tremble. He wags his
tail. If he would only always wag his tail I think
I would keep him. With deep hypocrisy I continue saying, "Good dog," and "Poor fellow,"
while I unfasten his chain.

He is loose. He barks. He larks. He gambols and capers. He makes straight for the centre
bed—the pride of ROSE ANNA'S heart. He attacks a newly-planted rose-tree and hurls it to the
dust, and then proceeds to dig what I conclude to
be a grave for it with his fore-paws. Ha, ha! A
hideous revenge — it shall hide his own car-
case!

I alter my conciliatory "Good dog" to a fero-
cious "Get out!" He thinks I'm calling him, and
comes up wagging his tail.

I repeat, "Get out!" more ferociously, and
make a kick at him. He retreats, still wagging
his tail.

I throw a stick at him, hoping it will kill, or, at
all events, stun him. It doesn't even hit him. He
picks it up in his mouth, brings it back, and lays it
at my feet, wagging his tail harder than ever.

I throw the stick away.   He runs after it (over two flower-beds), and again brings it back.

This is not to be borne.   I have experienced slights ever since I have taken up my abode in HIGHLOW Terrace.   I have been insulted by the dissolute youth over the way.   I have been victimized by the policeman.   I have been reproached by ROSE ANNA and sniggered at by MARIA.   I thought to manage a wife and a house, and I can't even control a dog !

I shout at him, " Be off! Get out !"

He shows symptoms of taking the hint, and is slinking off towards the road.   Ha, ha ! Now I will show him who is master.   I seize a flower-pot and hurl it at him.   It hits him.   He yelps.   I follow suit with another.   He howls.

The neighbours' windows begin to fill with heads, and I hear a voice say, " What a shame !"

I am reckless !—desperate !   I do not heed.   I exhaust the flower-pots, and scatter them all over the place, and then take to the ornamental shells with which ROSE ANNA has made what she calls a grotto.

The first one I throw misses Carlo, and goes through a window.   The neighbours laugh.   The dog retreats slowly   I fire a parting salute of shells and pebbles as he disappears out at the garder gate.   Victory !

I go in to breakfast. ROSE ANNA asks what I
have been doing. I am afraid to tell her. She
values the dog for her dear aunt's sake. Besides,
she may think it unkind of me to have broken so
many flower-pots and spoilt the grotto.

I am just beginning my coffee when ROSE
ANNA jumps up from her seat.

"Oh, here's poor Carlo at the window!"

He *is* there, and he wags his tail more vigorously than ever.

I rush at him; he rushes at me. He thinks I
have been having a game at larks with him, and
wants to renew the game.

There is only one course open to me. At the
end of HIGHLOW Terrace is a brickfield, and in that
brickfield a pond, and in that pond shall Carlo find
a watery grave.

I leave my unfinished meal, and lead him by
his chain into the brickfield. I reach the edge of
the pond, and tie a brick in my pocket-handkerchief, and fasten it to his collar. How to get him
into the water is the next consideration.

While I deliberate, he breaks from me, and
plunges into the pond; swims across, brick and all,
and swims back again.

He returns to me and shakes himself. I am
spattered from head to foot with muddy water
That dog must die!

He jumps upon me, and leaves the marks of his clayey paws on my new light waistcoat. I add another brick.

I try to fasten a third to his tail, but he won't stand it.

A man comes up. Do I want to drownd the dog?

I do.

Do I mind giving half-a-crown to any one as would do it for me?

I do.

I give half-a-crown, and leave this man engaged in intricate manipulation with the handkerchief and the bricks; for on consulting my watch, I find I have only just time, by taking a Hansom, to get to COUTER and PHLIMSY'S by the appointed hour. As it is I get there late, and get a wigging.

I have not time to stop for CARLO'S death struggles; but I hear a splash and a yelp as I leave the field. His doom is sealed, and a load is taken off my mind.

At the usual hour in the evening I return to HIGHLOW Terrace. I open the gate. A bark—a too familiar bark—salutes my ear.

I go round to the back, and find CARLO wagging his tail and entangling himself in his chain, and nearly tumbling over backwards with delight at my return.

I pat him. It is CARLO himself, and not his ghost. He is damp, but evidently in high spirits.

ROSE ANNA greets me with reproaches. How *could* I go and lose the dog—her dear aunt's present? How could I let him break away from me?—and what a fortunate thing it was I had tied my handkerchief round his neck, or he would never have been seen again.

I disguise my feelings. I ask for an explanation. I get it. In the afternoon a common-looking man had brought CARLO to the house. He said he had found him wandering about the brick-field, and had known whose he was by seeing the name of FULLALOVE on the handkerchief.

He demanded five shillings for bringing him back.

"Did you pay it?" I say, horror-struck.

"Of course," answers ROSE ANNA, complacently.

Thus, then, had seven-and-sixpence departed! But the day of reckoning is near at hand. A deadly drug shall be purchased, then—at the midnight hour!

    *   *   *   *   *

I am ill at ease. Married life, especially if you keep a dog, is not all bliss. I cannot sit on a mossy bank and play upon a pipe, while ROSE ANNA tends her sheep or catches butterflies. Per-

3

haps if I had a mossy bank I shouldn't do so; and, of course, I should have to learn the pipe before I could play. What I mean to say is that the stern realities of existence come upon me hourly, and the day-dreams of my happy and innocent bachelorhood are momentarily fading away.

But a truce to philosophizing. I have taken an oath, and the moment has arrived when a blow must be struck.

It is early morn; AURORA tips the opposite chimney-pots. I rise stealthily, and am careful not to wake ROSE ANNA. A quarter of a mile off is a chemist's shop. I hie me thither with speed and caution.

When I arrive, I am pale and haggard. My eyes are wild, and my speech is hesitating. No wonder, for I am out of breath.

I ask how much prussic acid will kill a man.

The chemist tells me.

I ask for enough to kill two men.

I will make sure of CARLO this time.

The chemist stares. He hesitates. He asks me questions. He disappears into the back shop, and closes the door of communication.

Presently I am conscious of an eye at one corner of the muslin curtain drawn across the glass. Then of another eye at the other corner. I am observed. I must dissemble.

I try to look careless, and whistle. I never could whistle, though; and find just now my attempts are rather worse than usual. I put on a dégagé air, and knock down a scent-bottle with my elbow.

This fetches the chemist out. He says if it's only a dog I want to kill, he has some stuff that will do it.

I say, What does he mean by "only a dog?"

He says he understood me at first to say two dogs.

I say "Oh," and ask how much?

It is sixpence, and the scent-bottle is a shilling. I pay him and go.

Looking round when I get to the street corner, I see the chemist at the shop door, speaking earnestly to a youth, and pointing towards me. Having turned the corner, I stand still, and a moment afterwards the youth turns it with rapidity, and comes face to face with me. I confront him.

I say, "Well?"

He says, "Well."

I say, "Do you want me?"

He says, "No, I don't," and walks on. I rather wish I had not spoken to him, and walk on too.

Owing to the long delay, ROSE ANNA has arisen during my absence. The cause of CARLO'S death must be a secret, and I must therefore defer

my vengeance until I return from the office. Presently I will put away the drug in a place of safety.
Meanwhile, breakfast.

The youth who followed me is strolling in front
of the house. It is evident he thinks I meditate
self-murder. The notion does not anger me. I
am amused, and humour his deception.

I walk to the window and assume a thoughtful
attitude. I tap my brow and smile vacantly.
Then I start and gaze wildly at the opposite houses.

In doing so, I observe that, as usual, the neighbours are deeply interested in my affairs, and that
one has got an opera glass. I therefore desist, and
finish my breakfast.

It is growing late. I put on my hat and set
off at a run. There is an omnibus just passing the
end of the road. I run after it and jump inside.
A moment later the youth climbs on to the roof.

When I get down at COUTER AND PHILIMSY'S
the youth also descends. I cast a wild and terrified glance at him, and enter the bank. I then
assume my office coat, and become a rational
being. There is a good deal to do to-day, and I
soon forget all about the matter.

Presently, however, I think of CARLO. What
did I do with the bottle of poison ? Did I leave
it on the breakfast table ? If so, will ROSE ANNA
mistake it for squills ?

It is impossible to go on working with this on my mind : I ask to leave early.

Mr. SIMPSON says, "You are always leaving early, FULLALOVE."

I say I must to-day : I am ill. He says, " What's the matter ?" I say, " Something wrong with my head." He looks at me strangely, and stealthily removes the ruler from my reach.

I am at home at last. I ask after ROSE ANNA. She is very poorly, MARIA says. I rush into the parlour. ROSE ANNA sits in a chair, propped up by pillows. What has happened ?

I am about to fling myself at her feet when my eye rests on the bottle of poison on the mantelpiece, evidently just as I left it, untouched. Upon this I laugh loudly.

ROSE ANNA bursts into tears. " How can you be so unfeeling ?" she says.

I say, "What's the matter?" She replies, " Don't you see how bad my cold is ?"

When ROSE ANNA and I have made it up again, I steal away and mix my deadly compound with choice scraps and savoury morsels. This I take to CARLO, who wags his tail with delight. With deep hypocrisy I say "Good dog—poor fellow," and watch him bury his muzzle in the poisoned mess. I do not leave him till I have seen him lick up every morsel. He wags his tail still, but I fancy with less energy than before.

The drug is already beginning to act. I leave him with a feeling of compassion, and spend the evening picturing to myself his death agonies. The last thing at night I listen at the back door under pretence of " locking up."

All is quiet.

In the middle of the night ROSE ANNA and I are startled from our sleep by a succession of deep barks. The brute is not dead yet, but must be at his last gasp. Still, for a dying dog, the noise is considerable. ROSE ANNA wants me to go and see what is the matter.

I don't tell her that I know. I feel I am an awful scoundrel, and shiver.

After a while there is a terrific howl. Then a deathlike silence. CARLO is no more !

Hardly, however, have I composed myself to sleep, when a loud and prolonged knocking sounds upon our street door. Hastily I shuffle on a few things, and throw open the window.

"What's the matter ?"

" Robbers ! Come down directly !"

ROSE ANNA screams. I am afraid I tremble. My wife presses the poker tenderly into my hand. " Go down and kill them, dear," she says.   •

I go down, but have my doubts about the killing.

I find a horrid-looking ruffian in the custody of two policemen, with CARLO smelling suspiciously round him, and occasionally playing with a bit of cloth exactly matching, in pattern, with the trousers of the burglar.

The ruffian had tried to break into our house, and CARLO had done his best to warn us. I am sorry I've given that dog poison. We wouldn't be warned, so with a sudden plunge he broke his chain, caught the robber's leg in his mouth, and held him fast till the policeman relieved him of his charge. I am very sorry that dog's doom is sealed.

I ask the policeman if he can get me a stomach pump. He doesn't think he can.

I go back to ROSE ANNA with a weight on my mind. I feel I have behaved badly to CARLO. Poor fellow! He will be stiff and cold by morning light.

By morning light I go to look at his body. I find it as animated as ever I don't understand it. CARLO must have a wonderful constitution.

While I am still wondering, a figure appears at the garden gate. It is the chemist of whom I bought the poison yesterday. He comes in. He is very cool. He says he hopes no offence, and he's very sorry; but I looked so strange and wild, and asked for such a quantity of prussic acid, that he was afraid to serve me, and gave me some coloured water instead of poison.

I bless him fervently He adds, that having learnt his mistake, he has come to apologize and to bring me genuine prussic acid. He wishes to know whether he shall give it to the dog ?

I tell him not for the world. I hug CARLO, who is astonished. I shake hands with the chemist, who stares. I laugh and sing, and bring on ROSE ANNA'S headache again.

Henceforth CARLO and I are sworn friends,

Death only shall part us !

Once more I am happy !

HOW SHALL WE SPEND OUR HOLIDAY?

Suggestion the first—Shopping.   Negatived decidedly.
N.B.—Married men, don't go, but do likewise.

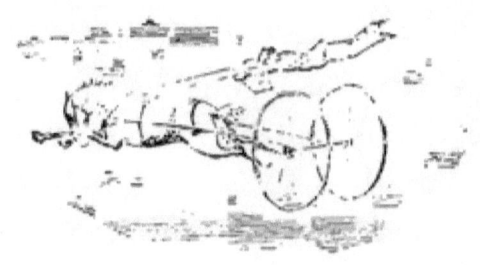

CHAPTER VI

I HIRE A GIG, AND SPEND A ROARING EVENING.

JOY!

COUTER and PHLIMSY have given me a holiday. They say it doesn't matter much whether I come to business or not. I hope they don't mean anything uncomplimentary. Well, if they do, what matters? They have given me the holiday.

Joy!

I discuss with ROSE ANNA how the holiday is to be spent. Suggestion the first — Shopping. Negatived decidedly.

Suggestion the second—Crystal Palace. Left open. Suggestion the third—Country lanes and shady groves, shepherdesses, crooks, and that sort of thing.

Mud presents an obstacle. Splashed white stockings are not romantic. With respect to groves, there is a shady one just at the back of our Terrace. It is called Todger's Grove, and is very shady indeed.

Fourth suggestion, by ROSE ANNA, pettishly— "Walk backwards and forwards all day between Highlow Terrace and COUTER and PHLIMSY'S."

I say "Pshaw!" and after a pause add "Tush!" Then I reflect. The result of my meditation is that I hit upon a brilliant notion. (There's more in my head than some people give me credit for.) We will go for a drive! we will have a pony-chaise, and explore the unknown land beyond the brick-field.

"But can you drive?" asks ROSE ANNA, doubtingly.

I answer indignantly, "Of course." (I suppose I can, but I've never tried; however, it seems easy enough.)

We send MARIA to order the vehicle. While she is gone we attire ourselves in our best; and as soon as we are ready "the carriage" comes to the door. It comes in the custody of a ragged boy, who drives, while MARIA sits by his side and grins all over her head.

This is not altogether as imposing as I could wish.

I help ROSE ANNA in and take my seat. I'm just a little bit nervous, I confess. I drop the whip. The pony shows symptoms of uneasiness

"Don't pull the reins so precious tight," says the boy; "you'll sor 'is yed off."

I must show that boy I know something about horses and their management. I say, "Boy, hadn't you better curb that snaffle up a bit?"

He grins, and remains silent. I hope I'm all right in the technicalities. Should it be "curb the snaffle" or "snaffle the curb?" Should it be either?

After some reflection I repeat my first suggestion, and then he says he thinks it's all right enough. I hope it is. In fact, I don't exactly see why it shouldn't be. Then he says, "Ichk!" or something like it, and the pony starts off before I know where I am. Presently I find I am on the seat, with one leg in the air, something like I should have been if I had caught a crab while rowing.

Suddenly ROSE ANNA says, "I've forgotten my parasol. Stop the horse!"

I call out, "Wo!" but the quadruped takes no notice. I call "Way!" rather louder, and tug at the reins. Perhaps I tug a little unevenly, for the pony veers round, and gets his fore feet upon the pavement.

I think at first he is going into one of the gardens—an idea which is shared by the garden's proprietor, who calls out, "Hallo! where are you coming to?"

I have no notion, and pull away at the reins harder than ever. We seem to be waltzing, and ROSE ANNA is growing alarmed. Providently the ragged boy comes to the rescue, and we come to a standstill.

ROSE ANNA sends for the parasol, and we wait patiently for its coming—the boy still holding the pony's head. Thank goodness, the parasol comes at last, just as a crowd is collecting.

" Let go his head," I say. I've heard this on an omnibus, and am certain it's all right. The boy lets go accordingly, and we start again.

One thing I must allow—when the pony does go, it goes. We are coming to the end of the road. I wonder what one ought to do when one wants a pony to turn a corner.

I wonder, if I leave him to himself, whether he'll run full tilt against the opposite railings. He relieves me of my anxiety by turning the corner so sharply that the carriage is nearly upset. ROSE ANNA tells me not to do it like that again, and I promise I won't.

He is a wonderful pony, and saves me all the trouble of driving. He goes by himself, turning and winding about in a marvellous manner. I wonder where he is taking us, and whether we shall ever find our way back again.

Presently we come out into the high road, just

in front of an omnibus. It seems a wonder to me we are not underneath it. Looking down at us, the driver says, "Where are you running to, stupid?" I glare up at him, but make no reply. The conductor adds, "Take him home, sir, and chain him up."

They say other things, and I see ROSE ANNA looks uncomfortable. I know I feel so, and wish they would drive on. Somehow the beast of a pony will keep up with them, and won't get on ahead.

All at once, however, he turns a corner of his own accord, and we escape. We are soon afterwards clear of the houses and in a long muddy lane. ROSE ANNA drops her parasol and bids me stop.

I call out "Wo!" as before; also "Way!" and as before he takes no notice of me. I pull viciously at the reins, and continue calling out "Way!" with the same effect, while ROSE ANNA calls "Hi!" and "Stop!"

The lane is growing narrower. There are deep cart-ruts, in and out of which we wobble most unpleasantly. Good gracious! how will this end?

In front a five-barred gate bars further progress. ROSE ANNA does not seem to understand that the pony is having it all his own way, and says, "Take care of the gate."

My sentiments are, let the gate take care of itself. Still, still he urges on his wild career. I shut my eyes and prepare for the worst, when suddenly the pony stops of his own accord, and I nearly go over the splash-board on to his back. ROSE ANNA thinks I just pulled him in in time. I do not undeceive her, but I go back for the parasol.

When I have got it we look things in the face. The lane is so narrow turning seems impossible, while further progress is effectually barred by the gate. At the hazard of our lives we must do something. It stands to reason we cannot remain in the muddy lane till somebody comes to fetch us.

ROSE ANNA says, very decidedly and rather crossly, "Turn round and go back." It's all very well talking, but how's it to be done? I make ROSE ANNA get out. She does, and complains of the mud. Perhaps there is cause, for it is over the tops of my boots.

I try to make the pony go backwards. He rises on his hind legs and dances. By-and-by he comes down on all-fours again, and I repeat the attempt. He backs viciously into a hedge. I say, "Come up!" and address him with the monosyllable "Gee!" He evidently does not understand horsey language. He is a duffer.

I deliberate. ROSE ANNA wants to know if she's to stand in the mud all day, and says, " Why don't you use the whip ?"

I use the whip, and with great effect. The pony starts violently, pulls the chaise out of the hedge, and sets off down the lane at a gallop. I follow, shouting " Hi !" and " Wo !" but he won't wo, and goes faster, and at last I lose sight of him altogether.

I go back for ROSE ANNA. I find her in tears. She reproaches me. There is nothing for it but to walk back. We have no notion where we are. The mud is almost unfathomable in some places, and I am encumbered with a whip, which, coupled with our splattered draggle-tailed appearance, tells our story to everyone we meet.

ROSE ANNA is in one of her worst tempers.

ROSE ANNA grows more peevish. She says she *won't* walk the length of HIGHLOW Terrace that figure, and be the laughing-stock of the whole neighbourhood. She says we must walk about the fields till dark.

I say we must not do anything of the sort, but in the end we do, for we lose our way and don't get home till eight o'clock, famished and fatigued.

We find the proprietor of the pony-chaise, with part of a broken shaft in his hand, waiting for us, and haranguing MARIA and all those of the neighbours who care to listen to the nature of the appalling accident which has, in all probability, befallen us.

Coming suddenly upon the scene, we cause somewhat the same effect as though we had been our own ghosts.

It appears that the pony went home, but smashed the chaise on his way. We then go into the question of the expense. I promise it shall be settled in a day or two ; and, when I am alone, ask myself how ? and feel poorly.

* * * * * *

It is a quarter to ten o'clock, and, just as I am turning out the gas, there comes a long loud double knock at the street door.

ROSA ANNA and I have had a few words half an hour ago, and she has gone to bed with a bad headache.

I stand on the mat hesitating, and wonder who it is. Then I draw the bolts, with some misgivings. A voice outside asks me if I am going to keep a fellow standing there all night. I recognize the voice, and devoutly wish I could keep it on the other side for ever. It is ROSE ANNA'S big-bearded, bullying, brutal, blustering brother.

I hear him strike a vesuvian on my new paint, and I smell tobacco as I turn the key.

I groan inwardly, for I know what I have to expect. He is a gentleman of wild and irregular habits, and in the old days when I went courting was given to the use of most insulting epithets with reference to myself.

" Now then, stupid !" he says, as I fumble with the latch. Then I open the door, and he steps into the passage and shakes a shower of rain off his shaggy coat on to me and my wall-paper. I know him of old, and expect he will hit me a great thump on the back—a thing I hate ; and so I take care to keep my face to him while we shake hands. Presently I turn to lead the way, and then he hits me.

He says, " Hallo, my early rooster, you're never going to bed at this time, surely ?"

I don't see why I shouldn't be ; but I reply, " Not for a minute or two."

He says, " That's all right. I'll stop an hour with you. Let's light up the gas."

After he has done so he sets to work to put the coals on the fire, which I have just removed with great care and a pair of tongs. He also puts on a fresh lump and breaks it with the poker. Then he bids me go and fetch ROSY. When I am halfway upstairs I hear him at the cheffonier, rattling the decanters.

I put it to ROSE ANNA. I say, " What's to be done ? ' She takes it as a matter of course. " Dear

fellow!" she says, " I'll be down in a moment.
Make him comfortable."

We find him, when we go down stairs again,
stretched on our new chintz-covered sofa, his
muddy boots resting on a cushion worked for us
by my sister ; and from his mouth come huge
volumes of rank tobacco smoke. Never before
has our little room been so profaned. I cough
violently, while ROSE ANNA, rushing to her brother, folds his burly form in her little arms.

He responds lazily. He says he is dead beat.
He has come up our way to see a fellow he knows,
and found him out. He goes on to remark that
he does not think much of our house, and wonders
what induced us to take it. Then he asks for a
tumbler, hot water, sugar, lemon, and a teaspoon,
adding as an afterthought, " and the gin bottle."
When he hears there is no lemon, he scoffs.

ROSE ANNA would not let *me* smoke—even if
I could—in the drawing-room. She would not let
my muddy boots rest on the clean chintz. But
who am I ? Nobody !

They treat me as such, and carry on a conversation without reference to me, while I play about
in the background. Under these circumstances I
do not exactly know how to comport myself. I
feel I am not taking that position in my own house
to which the payment of its rent entitles me.

I should like to assert my authority, only I
don't know how. ROSE ANNA and her brother
draw their chairs close to the fire, shutting me out
altogether, and take no further notice of me.

I take up a book and pretend to read. It is
Plutarch's Lives, and I can't do it. I endeavour to
collect my scattered senses, and have a vague idea
of sneaking off to bed. Indeed, I have lit a bed-
candle when ROSE ANNA stops me.

"I must go to bed now. You two gentlemen
make yourselves comfortable."

She says this with a smile ; but outside, in the
passage, she assumes a commanding tone.

"I insist that you behave properly to my
brother."

As she says this there is something about the
look of her eye which is almost terrible, and which
puts me in mind of Queen ELIZABETH in one
of CRUIKSHANK'S illustrations to The Tower of
London.

I say, "Of course, dear," and return to the
parlour, a little cowed ; but, soon, rage rises in my
bosom.

I try to be civil, and talk to ROSE ANNA's
brother. He yawns in my face. He says, "I'm
dead sleepy." I say, "Why not get home and go
to bed ?" He replies, "It's so jolly early yet ;" and
adds, "I feel inclined, too, for a roaring evening !"

I am in one of my sarcastic moods, and say, "Let's roar!" He replies, "What a muff you are!"

I curl up, and smoulder.

Presently, I hear a regular sound, and look towards him. He has gone to sleep. I say, "Hallo!"

He wakes up, and says, "Hallo!" also; then goes to sleep again.

My rage has now grown tremendous, and I am resolved on a terrible vengeance. He is fast asleep now. I rattle the fire-irons, and can't wake him. Then I smile to myself, and begin my work.

I noiselessly open the clock on the mantelpiece, and turn on the hour-hand to *four*. (It is in reality, half-past eleven.) Then I remove the coals from the fire, and put the fire out with the water from the kettle. Then I extinguish the gas, and light a bed-candle. Then I creep out into the passage, and take off my boots, coat, waistcoat, and collar, and I also tumble up my hair.

Then I open the parlour door again, suddenly, and rush in, and call out, "Hallo!"

ROSE ANNA'S brother springs up, and echoes the cry.

I say, yawning, "Didn't you call?" He replies, "No," and looking about wildly, adds, "What time
• :.)"

I yawn again, and show him the clock.

"Good gracious!" he says. "Why didn't you wake me?"

"I didn't like to," I reply; "you seemed so comfortable."

"I must be off!" he cries; and I show him out, and lock the door, and chuckle.

I go, chuckling, up to bed; and still chuckle when I have drawn the bed-clothes over my ears. But presently there is a tremendous rat-tat-tat at the door. He must have found out the trick and come back!

There has been unpleasantness. It *was* ROSE ANNA'S brother. He spoke his mind at the top of his voice before he went away. ROSE ANNA and I have had words and are reconciled. It is agreed that bygones shall be bygones, and so they are thus far.

*　　　*　　　*　　　*　　　*

CHAPTER VII.

WE GO IN FOR GARDENING—ROSE ANNA COOKS
THE DINNER, AND MY MOTHER'S SERVANT
SUSAN SETS US "TO RIGHTS."

ROSE ANNA has just said that we are a disgrace
to the neighbourhood. I have no doubt we
are, though I don't know why; but we have been
married long enough for me to understand the folly
of contradicting her. I agree, and after a pause
ask her the reason. She says, "Look at our garden."

I do look at it. I see a large crop of weeds. I
see the ruined grotto, the shells of which lie scattered
about as they fell when I pelted the unfortunate
Carlo. I see a large hole which the aforesaid
Carlo has dug with his fore paws, and some half-
dozen dismal-looking shrubs; and I am forced to
acknowledge we have not made the most of the
few feet of land of which I am the proud, and was
once the happy, owner.

ROSE ANNA A LA WATEAU.

(Only, because of the neighbours' windows, we did not carry out the notion. Rose Anna, as she really looked in her gardening gloves, and an ugly, is reserved for a future edition!)

She says decisively " Lay out the grounds."   Won't it cost a deal of money ?   She thinks not.

I ask ROSE ANNA what is to be done. She says, decisively, "Lay out the grounds." "Won't it cost a deal of money?" She thinks not. Further on, on being questioned as to what would be required, she says, with much emphasis, "A spade, a rake, a hoe."

I add, "A pick-axe and a bill." This is one of my jokes. ROSE ANNA doesn't see it, and tells me not to be foolish. Finally we decide upon making our thirtieth part of an acre look as park-like as possible, and we go in heavily for seeds, cuttings, bulbs, evergreens, and fruit-trees. ROSE ANNA says something about having a dress on purpose to conduct the operations, but I take no heed of this.

It is Saturday, and I come home early on purpose to assist in planting. My appearance in the wilderness, which is soon to be transformed into a little Paradise, armed with a huge spade and followed by ROSE ANNA, who brandishes a long rake, at once attracts the attention of the neighbours, and I see the windows commanding a view of the proceedings rapidly filling with eager faces. I get on pretty well with the evergreens, but at this time of year, when there are no leaves by which to distinguish the bushes, indeed, not even as much as to mark the difference between roots and branches, I begin to get a little uncertain.

There is one particular shrub which, from the long name appended to it, I conclude to be extremely choice. This I determine shall grace the little plot which separates our house from the road.

Our appearance in the front is a signal for all those children who are trundling their hoops and making an uproar, as is their custom of an afternoon, to cease their gambols, and hook themselves on to our railings.

They look on with awe and wonder, while I dig a deep hole; and when ROSE ANNA appears bearing the long-named bush, a cry of delight breaks from the crowd, who appear to expect some sort of conjuring trick.

Attracted by the crowd, a couple of bricklayers passing on the other side cross over and watch the proceedings with much interest. "That'll grow, Bill, won't it?" says one with a laugh, as ROSE ANNA puts the bush in the hole, and I proceed to shovel in the earth.

I am seized with a sudden dread. I inquire of ROSE ANNA in a whisper whether she heard the satirical remark. She did. Can she explain it? She can't. Does she think we've put the tree the wrong end up? She doesn't know.

I feel that my dignity will suffer if I allow a plant to remain in sight of every passer-by with its roots in the air and its branches in the ground. I have no notion, however, which is which. The fool of a nurseryman ought to have labelled the shrubs, " This side up."

I pull the beastly thing out again hastily, and say, " Come along," to ROSE ANNA. She comes along. The spectators all laugh. ROSE ANNA says I am making her the joke of the neighbourhood, and shows symptoms of crying.

To console her, I tell her I will show the gaping idiots that we know what we are about, so will go and plant some bulbs. There can be no mistake about their ends; though, now I look at them, I'm not so sure of that either. However, I go at the work boldly.

I dig a multitude of small holes and put the bulbs in. The bricklayers are still there, and are whispering together. They appear to extract great amusement from our gardening operations. I wish they would go away, but don't suppose it will be of any use to tell them to do so.

ROSE ANNA rakes the beds smooth. MARIA, under protest, waters them. I, with a smile of triumph, contemplate them. The children at the railings, led on by one of the bricklayers, give us a cheer as we enter our front door.

The next morning I wake early. I wonder if the bulbs have sprouted yet. ROSE ANNA thinks not, but says I'd better go and look. Horror!

Wherever I planted a bulb I find a hole. Some evilly disposed person has come in the night and robbed me of my flowers. I don't believe there is one remaining.

I rush back to ROSE ANNA, and tell her the news. She says it's all my fault, because I wouldn't plant the shrub with a long name. I say it's all hers, because she couldn't tell its head from its tail. She weeps. She says she never would have married me if she had thought I should have been so ruffianly. I melt, and we have a damp and miserable breakfast.

The shades of night are falling fast, when MARIA tells me a man wants to speak to me. The question is, "Do I want to speak to the man?" I survey him through the crack of the kitchen door, to see if I know who he is. I don't ; but he catches my eye, and says, "Come in, guv'nor, don't be afeard !"

I go in as majestically as I can, under the circumstances. He quails a bit ; then I recognise in him one of the bricklayers who leant over the railings the preceding day

I ask him what he wants : he says, "Would I like to buy any bulbs?" I think this question strange, coming from such a quarter; he says he has some, and produces them. I look at them. I believe they are mine, and it was he who stole them ; but one bulb is so like another, I should hardly like to swear to them. However, I say—

"Why, these are my own!" "Right you are, guv'nor," says the bricklayer, "if you like to give half-a-crown for them."

I explain, I don't mean that. I go on to say that the bulbs I planted on Saturday have been stolen. Bricklayer says, "Law!" and adds, "what a lot of rogues there are in the world!"

Emboldened, I say, "And I believe these are the very ones." He wants to know what I mean, so ferociously, that he takes away my breath. He asks if I dare accuse him, a 'onest, 'ard-working labourer, and a compound 'ouse-'older, of theft ?

He asks, indignantly, if a man who has got a vote is likely to steal, and suggests that I should apologise, adding, that he should prefer the apology taking the form of a " drop of sum'at 'ot."

I answer him, angrily, that I'll see him further first ; upon which he uses very objectionable language, threatens to smash the windows, to have me up before the Lord Mayor, to bring an action for defamation of character, and to throw me into Chancery. Then he goes out, banging the door after him with such force as to shake two plates off the shelf; and I hear him vowing vengeance, at the top of his voice, as he walks away.

I hope the matter will not go any further ; but I am afraid I have rather made an ass of myself in this little business.

*　　*　　*　　*　　*

Happiness at last !

Peace of mind ! Ease ! Comfort ! General joy ! MARIA has gone.

I feel I am now master of my own house. I proudly stride. I triumphantly straddle. I " take the stage," to use a theatrical expression. I put my thumbs into my waistcoat armholes and expand. I am " all there," as the saying is, which saying, to be more applicable, should be, " all here."

Yes, she is gone. Her month was not up. We had given her warning, and had made up our minds to get rid of her at the month's end ; but she went suddenly of her own accord, at the end of ten days, without intimating that such was her intention.

I awake in the morning, and wonder why I am not called. I flatter myself I have awakened too early. I turn over, with a grunt of satisfaction. There is nothing more delightful than to wake too soon and to doze off again.

But it is surprising how very wide awake I am ! I hope nothing is wrong. How can anything be wrong, though ? Whatever her other faults might be, MARIA was punctuality itself. I close my eyes, and sink into a blissful slumber. Then I awake again, very wide awake, indeed, and say to myself, "How strange this is !"

I consult ROSE ANNA. She, also, is wide awake, and of my opinion.

I reach out of bed, and pull the bell. There is no answer. I pull again. I go out on the landing. I bawl out, "MARIA!" The cat, shut in the kitchen, mews dismally, in answer to my call. Otherwise there is a death-like silence.

I am conscious of a trembling in the knees. It must be the cold. I go back to ROSE ANNA, and say, "Don't you think we ought to do something ?"

She says, "I think *you* ought."

I say, "What ?"

She doesn't know.

After some reflection, I go down stairs, and find that MARIA has fled, and that the supper things are as we left them. I also find that it is nearly an hour and a half later than my usual hour of getting up ; and the thought of COUTER AND PHLIMSY'S wrath drives all other ideas out of my head.

Further investigations prove that MARIA has not robbed us very much, as far as we are able to ascertain, though things generally seem all to be missing. It appears that she has gone away with that soldier I found in the kitchen. A "writing" to that effect, found upon the kitchen table, explains matters. The style seems founded upon the literature of the halfpenny weekly journals, but she spoils her good intentions by spelling honourable without an "h," and signing her name with a small "m."

Anyhow, she has gone, and I hope never to see her grinning face again. The only drawback to perfect enjoyment is, that her successor has not made her appearance, and we are obliged to "do" for ourselves in the meantime.

ROSE ANNA is inclined to take a cheerful view of things, and says, "We must get on, anyhow."

At the end of the first day it is my impression that we are not getting on at all ; but I don't like to mention it, and console myself for my miseries with the reflection that we've seen the last of MARIA.

The first day we have not done much in the way of cookery, but have subsisted, for the most part, on things from the cook-shop. Sitting in a room without a fire, (it has gone out, and it is such a trouble to light it up again) ; and eating dinner without a table-cloth, because it has been put away somewhere in a hurry ; and without any beer, because I forgot to order it—I venture to express an opinion that things are not as comfortable as they might be.

Rose Anna says, "It's as good as a picnic."

I say "Hang picnics?" and Rose Anna bursts into tears, and says, "How can you be so selfish?"

We have some more unpleasantness after this, and Rose Anna sits and sulks among the dirty plates. Later on we make it up, and have some hot gin-and-water out of the same tumbler.

We find, when we want to go to bed, that there are no more candles in the house, and we can't carry the gas upstairs. Rose Anna says, " Never mind," and we don't ; only I bump my toe against something in the dark.

The course of high-dried salt beef we have been going through makes me dreadfully thirsty at dead of night ; but I find that we forgot to fill the water-jug. I have an idea of going down in the dark to get water from the back kitchen ; but the thought of the black beetles dispirits me, and so I go to bed again instead, and try to forget what I wanted.

Next day, as I shave (with cold water), I ask myself, "Would it be a manly act on my part to pretend I was kept late at the office, and dine out?" On reflection, it appears that it wouldn't, and I groan as I think of the cold boiled beef.

Rose Anna, at breakfast, has a notion. Her

mother spoke yesterday of a servant she could get for us. In the meantime a charwoman from the neighbourhood will come in to assist, and ROSE ANNA feels certain she can get on capitally.

She says, with one of her sweetest smiles, "You don't know what a good cook I am."

I confess I don't, and I go away to the city with sundry misgivings, and with a feeling in my heart that if I am hungry I had better take a snack on the way home. I *am* awfully hungry ; but I am afraid of venturing on the snack for fear of detection. Tears, reproaches, and big brothers would be my doom, and I refrain.

On opening the street door I smell a smell of burning. There is also a prodigious sound of frying. ROSE ANNA comes out from the kitchen, looking very black about the face and hands, otherwise in the best of spirits, and says, "You're early, aren't you ?"

I am about half an hour late. I say, "No ; I'm hungry, though."

She says, "You dear, it's nearly ready ;" and seizing me round the throat, forgets she has still got the cooking-fork in her hand, with which she pricks the back of my head. "What's it smell like ?"

I secretly think, "Tallow candles ;" but deceitfully reply, "Something good, I'll bet a penny."

" It's my first attempt," she answers ; "and that's such a horrid oven we've got. You can cook nothing in it."

I go into the parlour and wait. Some time elapses. I grow hungrier and hungrier.

More time elapses. I begin to feel rather faint.

There are some sweet biscuits in the cheffonier. I eat one, and wait a little longer. The pangs of hunger urge me to eat another, then a third, and a fourth. I nearly empty the plate.

ROSE ANNA comes in suddenly, and finds me with my mouth full. I turn away and dissemble, for it strikes me all at once I'm doing rather a mean thing.

Dinner *is* ready at last, but ROSE ANNA has to apologize. While she was looking after the pudding the meat got burnt a little. But I won't mind ? Oh, no ; why should I ? I never recollect eating anything so dreadful, but I swallow a few charred lumps and make up with bread.

ROSE ANNA says, " You don't care about potatoes." I suppose not, as she says so ; anyhow, there are none.

The pudding follows. She waits till I have taken a spoonful, and says, " Well ?" hopefully.

I say, " Wait a minute," not so hopefully.

She says, " That ought to be good ; it cost enough."

I say, "Did it?" and try to taste it, as it were, in a new light, but it don't taste any nicer.

ROSE ANNA has a try, and then bursts into tears. I say, "Never mind, let's make up with cheese." There is no cheese, so we make up without it. We are happy again. ROSE ANNA says, "It's that stupid cookery book!" I add, "And the oven!"

Presently there comes a knock at the door. It is a middle-aged, steady-looking person, with a letter. She comes from my mother, to whom I had written, and my mother says she will just suit us.

I say to ROSE ANNA, "Isn't this capital!" ROSE ANNA don't seem too pleased, and replies, "But my mamma has got one, too!"

I say, "'Bird in the hand,' you know," and ask the middle-aged person when she can come.

"Now," she says.

I think this rather sudden, but still we want her as soon as possible. ROSE ANNA hangs back and looks blacker than ever. I hope the middle-aged person does not take her for another servant. I think so, but am afraid to mention it.

I say, "I'll show you the kitchen," and show it her.

She silently disapproves.

I say, "We are rather in a mess."

She says, " I think so, sir."

I say, " There's a very nasty smell."

She replies, " There's several, sir, I think !"

I suppose she means this for a joke, so I laugh faintly, and get back as soon as I can to the parlour. ROSE ANNA is waiting for me——

*   *   *   *

Our SUSAN—that's the new servant my mother sent us—seems to me to be every thing that we can desire. ROSE ANNA, unfortunately, does not appear to be of the same opinion.

SUSAN is middle-aged, and of staid and stern demeanour. She announces her attention of setting us to rights. She begins by setting us to wrongs ; that is to say, the first morning after her arrival, she piles all the furniture of each separate room in the middle, and is seen everywhere in company with steaming water, mops, and scrubbing-brushes.

ROSE ANNA does not see the occasion for this state of things, and tells SUSAN so. SUSAN contemplates her with a pitying expression, and appeals to me. To tell the truth, I rather like being appealed to. I have not been used to it, and I am glad to see a disposition on the part of our new servant to recognize my consequence.

I therefore tell her I think she is perfectly right.

ROSE ANNA bridles at this, but SUSAN pays no attention to her, and goes on piling up the furniture, and, presently, asks me for money to buy a broom.

She asks me in the passage, and I am going to give it her, when ROSE ANNA calls to me in terrible tones. I think it best to go, to avoid unpleasantness, but promise to come back. ROSE ANNA says, "We want no brooms." I reply, "SUSAN says—" She answers, "SUSAN, fiddlesticks!" I remark, "Just so."

ROSE ANNA goes on to say, speaking loud, as it seems to me, for SUSAN'S benefit, that she expects in the course of the day her dear mother will send us a servant. I observe that it will be very awkward if she does. She replies, "Not at all! SUSAN will have to go!" Upon which SUSAN, in the far distance, says, "Pooh!" and goes on scrubbing.

About this period it occurs to me I might as well go to the City, and do so by the back door, thus getting very neatly out of the broom difficulty. When I come home again at night, SUSAN is still scrubbing. The house smells as if it were being boiled with soap-sauce. Its general appearance is damp and steamy, and ROSE ANNA is nowhere to be seen. I hunt for her, and am guided by a sneeze.

I find her in tears in the lumber-room, blocked up by boxes, looking cross and disheartened. She greets me with a sob, and indignantly desires to be informed whether she is the mistress of the house, or SUSAN.

I sit down on a box, and ask what is the matter. ROSE ANNA explains, at great length. The new servant, it seems, has chased her from room to room, throughout the day. Having been expelled from the little drawing-room by a cloud of dust, she had sought refuge in the still smaller dining-room, whence she had been forced to beat a hasty retreat across the steamy passage, and up the dripping stairs. But the demon of cleanliness, as she calls SUSAN, still pursued her.

She had remonstrated : SUSAN treated her with silent contempt. She commanded : SUSAN laughed, and said the master had told her to clean the house down. Thus, finally, ROSE ANNA had been thoroughly routed, and she now requests that I will instantly dismiss the woman.

I say, "Let's have dinner first." ROSE ANNA smiles bitterly, and we go down stairs and pull the bell. SUSAN appears damp and dishevelled, like an elderly mermaid. I tell her to bring up dinner as soon as possible.

She replies, "You don't want no dinner ; but you what I'll do——"

I repeat, in my quietly sarcastic way, "You'll tell me what, eh? What is it?"

"By-and-by, when I've done cleaning"—she goes on seemingly unconscious of the satire—"I'll run out and get you a bit of beef to eat with your tea."

I tell her, "This is absurd!" and that I must have my proper meals. She says, "You can't have no dinner, cos there ain't none for you to have;" and, without waiting for a reply, she goes down stairs, and I hear her scrubbing vigorously in the kitchen.

ROSE ANNA and I gaze blankly at each other. Endeavouring to put the best face on it, I point out to her how nice it will be when the house is thoroughly clean and dry again.

She sneezes in reply, and we sit in a species of vapour-bath longing for food.

Presently there comes a low single knock at the front door. SUSAN in the distance is still scrubbing, and, after a time, the knock is repeated. To save trouble, I answer the door. A very large, very fat, and very sturdy woman, in rusty black, with a bandbox in one hand and a carpet-bag in the other, says, with an expression of the deepest scorn, "Well, you've come at last," and forces her way past me into the passage.

I don't think I feel altogether sorry when she stumbles over a pail and—drats it.

She says to me, "Where's your mistress?" I explain to her with dignity who I am, but she does not appear to be impressed, and ROSE ANNA, hearing the conversation, comes out.

"Oh, PERKINS," she says, "I am so glad to see you. I thought you'd come."

"Time I did," says PERKINS; "you want a deal of setting to rights."

SUSAN comes forward and listens.

"I'll soon put you in order," says PERKINS.

"What's that you're saying?" asks SUSAN.

"Who is that?" asks PERKINS.

ROSE ANNA answers for her, and says to SUSAN, "This is our new servant, and you had better go."

Upon this SUSAN appeals to me. I said before I liked being appealed to, and I think, under the circumstances, I am bound to support the servant my mother sent; but yet I would prefer things should be amicably arranged.

I put it in this light to ROSE ANNA, who says decisively, "Turn her out of the house!"

I say, "My dear, that isn't the pleasantest way, is it?" She replies, "There is no other." I am sorry for this, because I confess I don't quite see how it is to be done.

Meanwhile there is an awful disturbance in the passage. Insulting language is used freely on either side. The sounds of a scuffle reach us, and of a panting for breath ; also a bumping noise, as of a head against a wall.

ROSE ANNA says, "They are killing one another. Go and separate them!"

I reply, calmly, "Let them have it out, and the one that survives we can keep."

But here the door is burst open, and the two combatants tumble in together, both looking very flushed and angry.

"If you please, mum, I should like to go," says PERKINS.

"I'll take my money, sir," says SUSAN.

*   *   *   *   *

PERKINS *has* gone, and SUSAN has had her money.

They are both gone, and we are still on the wrong side of dinner. ROSE ANNA is crying.

Our first dinner was not a success, nor indeed was the tea and a little music particularly cheerful.

This is another allegorical sort of picture. The figure in front represents the young lady at the pastrycook's as seen by the eyes of FUL-IMOVE. *Mrs. F., on the contrary, insists that the dark outline is much nearer the truth.*

CHAPTER VIII.

I CAN'T exactly say that we're quite settled yet.

We've got a girl to come on by the day, and a boy to come on by the night. They don't come on very regularly, and they break a good deal, and they are both great readers.

I find *Charley Wag* hidden away in the soup tureen, the *Cottage Girl* among the blacking brushes, and *Dare-Devil-Dick* in the frying-pan; but I can't find the cork-screw anywhere. I look for HENRY, our boy, and I don't find him either. Upon further search, I discover him at play in the road, and say, "If I catch you, my fine fellow——" I don't precisely know what I am going to do in that case; but as I don't catch him, it doesn't much matter.

I wish we *were* settled. For ever so long I have been telling my friends I hope to see them when we're settled. ROSE ANNA has been doing the same thing. It has at last become a sort of joke among my friends to ask me whether I'm settled yet. I don't see the joke myself, but *they* laugh at it.

ROSE ANNA says it's no use going on like this any longer, making ourselves ridiculous, and we *must* ask our friends. I remonstrate : she resists. I ask, " How about the cooking ?" She says, " Pastrycook." I say, " How about the waiting ?" She replies, " Greengrocer." In conclusion, I say, " How about the expense ?" and she answers, " Bother !"

Upon this we fix a day, and make our preparations. ROSE ANNA says, " Will you see JOHNSON ?" JOHNSON is the pastrycook in the high road, and there is a remarkably pretty girl who takes care of the counter. I say, " I will see JOHNSON" (meaning the pretty girl), and I see him— that is to say, her—that evening, and give **my** order.

I brush my hair at the parlour glass before going, and ROSE ANNA says, " How smart you are making yourself !" I say, " Not at all," and feel confused. She says, " You need not dress to run round there." (It is only a few doors off.) I reply, " Who is dressing ?" and after this don't like to stop to change my collar. When I get three doors from the house, I find I have left my gloves at home. However, it cannot be helped.

I trip along the road, and, as far as lies in my power, avoid the puddles. She is in the shop, and while I am struggling with the obstinate door-handle, she gazes at me through the window.

The door gives way suddenly, and I go in with a rush. This confuses me a little, and spoils the effect of my entrance. When I recover myself, I say, " Good evening, miss !" Nothing particularly brilliant occurs to me after this, so I give the order and come away. I am rather confused about some of the particulars, and would like to go back to tell her over again. I do come back as far as the door, and through the glass see her and the pastrycook laughing considerably. I rather fancy it is about my stumbling, so I go away again, and hope they didn't catch sight of me.

Next day I issue my invitations with a jaunty nonchalant air. I say, " POPKINS, old boy, come and take pot-luck with us to-day, will you ? That's right ; then I'll ask HOPKINS to meet you."

HOPKINS also is disengaged, so the three of us go down to HIGHLOW Terrace on the roof of the omnibus.

At our place everybody says POPKINS is a funny fellow. I hope ROSE ANNA will like him, but I have my doubts.

ROSE ANNA and her friends are waiting for us in the drawing-room, and it strikes me, when we go in, they are looking rather grim and stately.

I shake hands, and introduce HOPKINS and POPKINS. In the hurry of the moment, I call HOPKINS POPKINS, and POPKINS HOPKINS. Then finding out my mistake, I laugh, and try to correct it. This, if possible, makes matters more confusing, and from the way I have put it, I feel certain nobody but HOPKINS and POPKINS, themselves, have the remotest notion which is which.

After this there is a dead silence. I say, cheerfully, " We dine at seven." Simultaneous movement of everybody's head towards the clock ticking on the mantelpiece. A simultaneous murmur of satisfaction on finding it only wants ten minutes to the hour.

Second pause, and a silence more awful than the first. A remark that it has been very cold meets with no response. Confound POPKINS! If he wants to be comic, now's the time for it. I whisper to him, " Say something funny "

He asks back, with much mystery, " What ?"

I say, "Anything." Then aloud, "What was that riddle you asked us on the 'bus?" Everybody looks at him expectantly, and he begins. "Why is a——" Then he laughs. We all laugh encouragingly "Why is an ugly duckling——"

"Please, ma'am, I want to speak to you," says our girl, looking in at the door.

"I *must* hear what it is," says ROSE ANNA in a gushing way, referring to the riddle.

"We'll wait for you;" and ROSE ANNA leaves us waiting while she talks to the girl in the passage. They talk very loud, and there is a dead silence within the room, so that we hear all they say, but try to look as if we didn't. I have an idea of drowning the sound by some remark, but can't think of any.

Presently ROSE ANNA returns, looking put out and flurried.

"I was going to ask you a riddle," says POP-KINS, returning to the charge, and heading a forlorn hope of conversation with much courage, "I was going to ask you why an ugly——"

"I say, POPKINS," says HOPKINS; "it isn't that one about NAPOLEON, is it? because, you know, it—a—it isn't quite what one would like to say—before ladies."

Chorus of ladies, eagerly, "What is the one about NAPOLEON?"

" Let me see," says HOPKINS. " It's very good, but I'm sure I can't remember it. The answer is —Because he's a——. There, now, I forget the answer too. Never mind, POPKINS, go on. I shall think of mine presently."

POPKINS again :—" Why is an ugly duckling—"

" Must it be ugly ?"

" Yes, of course. Why is an ugly——"

But about this point I discover that ROSE ANNA is making signs to me to follow her out into the passage. I leave the duckling, and follow her out. I say, " Why don't we have dinner ?" She says, " It's not come." I say, " Send HENRY." She sends HENRY, and we go back into the drawing-room.

There is more conversation after this, and several pauses. ROSE ANNA is again summoned to the passage, and again *I* am summoned thither. She says, " The boy couldn't find the shop ; I've sent him again." I say, " We have made the soup at home, haven't we ?" "Yes," she replies. Then I say, " Let's begin."

ROSE ANNA thinks it would be best to wait for the other things ; but I say, " No, they're certain to be here in a moment ;" and we sit down.

They are, however, several moments, and yet do not arrive. We begin soup. We loiter over soup. Some of us have two helps. Finally we conclude soup, and the other things do not appear. I begin to grow hot and cold—conversation is impossible. I take ROSE ANNA into the passage, and say, "What's to be done?" She says, "Run round to the shop." I say, "In the middle of dinner?" She says, "Yes; what else can you do?"

I do not wait to ask; I go out at the back, and rush breathlessly to the pastrycook's. I ask the young lady there why the dinner is so late.

She says, "What dinner?"

I repeat, in frenzied tones, "WHAT DINNER?— OUR DINNER! The dinner I ordered for to-day at six o'clock!"

She replies very calmly, "*You ordered it for to-morrow, sir, not to-day.*" Then she opens a book. "Yes, sir, to-morrow. I wrote it down, sir, when you gave the order."

"You don't happen to have another dinner in stock?" I inquire.

"No, sir."

I come over suddenly very faint, and take a chair to save myself from falling. What on earth is to be done?

With visitors at home waiting for dinner, and every prospect of their having to wait till to-morrow before they get it, I am sitting here, limp and list-less, at the pastrycook's, wondering what I ought to do next.

The young lady seems surprised at my behaviour. She wonders why I don't go away, or buy something. She pushes the Bath buns towards me. I take one, and ask for a glass of cherry-brandy

I find the bun a little too cloggy, but the cherry-brandy is soothing, and I ask for more. I ask for more again. I wish to collect my thoughts, and look my difficulty in the face. Strange to say, the more cherry-brandy I take, the less collected my thoughts become.

The young lady regards me with interest, and asks if I am ill. I laugh incoherently, and she draws back alarmed, and shelters herself behind a big bottle-full of jumbles. I am thinking of my guests! I am picturing to myself the five miserable creatures sitting in my wretched parlour sipping at my awful soup.

They must by this time have been helped thrice. The tureen must be empty, and they are waiting hopefully for the next course!

The next course! When will that be? Next week, probably, if they will stop for it.

An idea occurs to me, slightly wild, perhaps, but yet an idea. Suppose I ask the pastrycook's young lady to elope with me! If we were to fill our pockets with Bath buns, fly to climes beyond the brick-field, and leave the miserable five to go on waiting for the second course until the end of time?

But this is folly. A rush of customers arrives. I am elbowed from my position, and I drag myself from the scene of my enchantment. In dragging myself away, I forget to settle for the bun and brandy, and am called after. I return and settle, and once more face my difficulties.

I still have notions of running away, but I have not the courage; besides, it wouldn't be quite the thing to leave ROSE ANNA in the lurch, so I go back home and let myself in noiselessly.

The servant-girl meets me, and implores me to say when the other courses are coming. I hiss in her ear, as they do in the tales in the *Halfpenny Journal*, "Silence, woman!" She shrinks back, silenced—probably appalled.

Left alone, I peep through the crevice of the dining-room door, which has been left ajar.

My object is to catch ROSE ANNA'S eye, call her out, and make a private explanation.

It is a dismal scene that I look in upon. There is my place—the place of the master of the house —at the head of the table, occupied by a spoon and a bit of bread. Opposite that spoon and bit of bread sits ROSE ANNA, bolt upright, and with a terrible expression of eye.

The gentlemen visitors are, I observe, mostly

playing with their knives; the lady visitors are, for the greater part, crumbling bread, and occasionally eating a few crumbs. The soup tureen is empty. So are the decanters. So are my guests.

I make subdued noises, to attract ROSE AN-NA'S attention, and am taken for the cat.

I tap, and am told to come in.

At last I catch ROSE ANNA'S eye, and make frantic pantomime to her to come out and speak to me.

She frowns angrily, and I repeat my gestures. She signs to me imperiously to come forward. I go through my contortions yet again. I see POPKINS has his eye on me. Also HOP-KINS.

ROSE ANNA loses patience, and cries aloud, petulantly, "For goodness' sake, do come in! What's the good of making faces like that?"

POPKINS sees an opportunity for one of his jokes. He is sitting near the door, and throws it wide open, disclosing me in an attitude of intense pantomime, and with an exaggerated agony on my face.

POPKINS says "Bravo!" and every one laughs, or tries to. Under the circumstances I think it best to pretend it *is* a joke, and so throw myself into another attitude, at which nobody laughs at all, and I come out of it feeling rather stupid.

Then ROSE ANNA says, "Now MR. FULLA-
LOVE, as soon as you have *quite* finished your
monkey tricks, perhaps you'll take your seat, and
behave like a gentleman."

I am greatly confused by this style of address,
and say, imploringly, "My dear ROSE ANNA——"

"There, there!" she continues, "we've had
quite enough buffoonery. Sit down, and eat your
dinner."

I inwardly writhe at this reproof, but I know
what ROSE ANNA is when she is roused, and think
it best not further to excite her. POPKINS, who is
on for some more of his foolery, also collapses, but
lunges at me with his leg under the table, and, as
it were, takes me into his confidence with a wink.

When, however, ROSE ANNA says, "Sit down,
and eat your dinner," I cannot refrain from a smile.
What dinner? I ask myself, and I sit down and
play with a bit of bread, and look at my face in the
spoon, and pretend to be expecting the next course
every minute.

But at last it has all to be told. There is no
next course, and no hope of any The company
are horror-struck. ROSE ANNA becomes hysterical.

POPKINS suggests stewing the table-cloth. One
or two mutter, "Bread and cheese," and I silently
wait for results.

At length one of the lady visitors comes to the

rescue. She calls it fun, and treats the affair as a joke. She proposes that she and ROSE ANNA should extemporize a little something eatable. They go to the kitchen, and we are left for a while to amuse ourselves with the breadcrumbs. We are not much amused, and find the conversation uphill work.

Finally a meal is served up, of which this is the " c'rect card "—

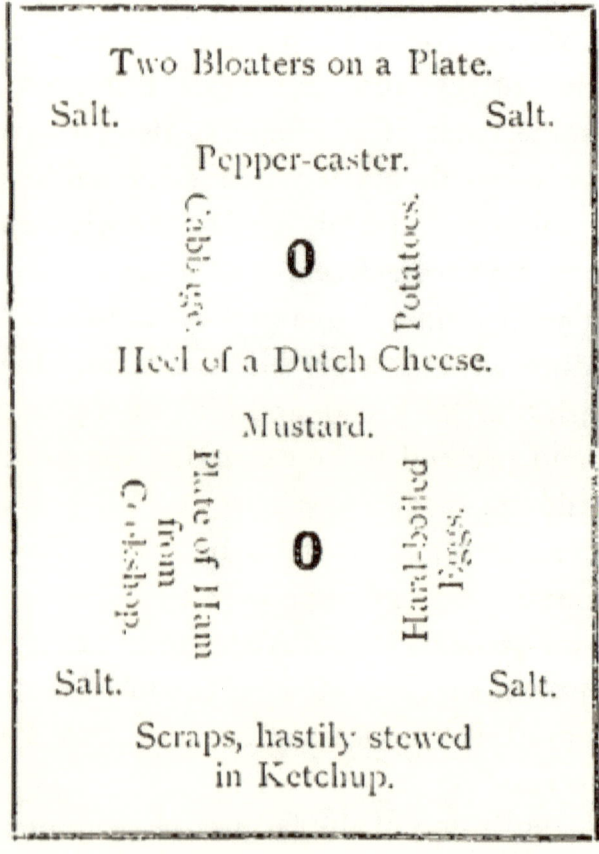

Two Bloaters on a Plate.

Salt.   Salt.

Pepper-caster.

Cabbage.   O   Potatoes.

Heel of a Dutch Cheese.

Mustard.

Cockshop. Plate of Ham O Hard-boiled Eggs.
from

Salt.   Salt.

Scraps, hastily stewed
in Ketchup.

The removes consist of a shillingsworth of Bath buns.

Altogether, our first dinner party is certainly not a success, nor, indeed, are the tea and the little music, which we have afterwards, particularly cheerful.

*   *   *   *   *

I must say I think ROSE ANNA is a little too severe on the subject of that dinner. Her remarks are withering, and I am not altogether sorry when the time comes for my departure for the City ; but on arriving at COUTER AND PHLIMSY'S, I find that I—to use a very appropriate expression—have got out of the frying-pan into the fire.

POPKINS has made the events of the evening into a comical story (I can't think what people see in POPKINS'S wit), and he has been telling it with great applause at the office before my arrival. I am greeted with a shout of laughter in consequence. What a donkey POPKINS is !

I say in my most sarcastic manner, that I don't believe half of them know what a dinner is. This is a crushing rejoinder, I fancy ; but though they never miss a point when POPKINS speaks, somehow or other they don't notice my clever sayings.

The fact is the rejoinders are too clever, too crushing, too scathing, for their common ill-educated

minds to appreciate ; they can only comprehend the
coarse fun of POPKINS, and the personalities of HOP-
KINS. Perhaps, when I am dead, some one will collect my repartees, and make a book of them—though
that is a poor consolation.   My day at COUTER AND
PHLIMSY'S is an unpleasant one, and when I turn
my back upon the office I shake an imaginary fist
at POPKINS, and jump into the first HIGHLOW
Terrace omnibus.

ROSE ANNA has quite recovered her serene and
placid temperament when I reach home.   She
welcomes me in the garden, and we go into the
house to dinner.   There is a dinner to-day, a joint
big enough for a dozen, but I am hungry, and eat
my share, perhaps a little more too.

We have just finished our meal when we
are startled by a loud knock at the street
door.

Presently there is a trampling of feet in the
passage, and in the distance I hear the sound of
many voices.   I ring for the temporary servant,
and ask for an explanation.   She says, if I please,
it's the man from the pastrycook's.   I spring from
my chair with unwonted agility, dart into the passage, and come into violent collision with a boy
bearing a tray upon his head.   There is a terrific
smash.   Amongst the ruins I descry portions of a
barley-sugar temple which has been the pride of

the pastrycook's window for many months. Bewildered, I rush into the kitchen.

Table and dresser are already loaded with dishes. I hurry back again, meeting another boy with another tray in the passage, and go to the front door.

Several ragged children are clustering about my front garden railings. Several neighbours' noses are glued to their respective window panes. The ragged children give a faint cheer as I emerge from the house and stand on the top step.

One, bigger than the rest, observes : his eyes, don't I look as if I wanted a good blow-out.

I am too bewildered to resent this insult. I look up the road and see a man and a boy, both with trays, coming towards my house, and while I gaze another man appears round the corner with another tray.

I am paralyzed, and perhaps should have continued so, only ROSE ANNA seizes my coat-tails, and in a stern voice commands me to come in. She wants to know the meaning of all this. I can't tell her. I suppose it's yesterday's dinner come to-day.

We go together to send back the trays and the men and boys.

The men and the boys go back without any sending—the trays don't.

A strong smell of savoury dishes fills the house.
I run round to the pastrycook's without stopping
to arrange my hair or to think of the young
lady.

She is very sorry, with a smile on her face, but
the dinner was ordered, and has been sent. She
can't think of taking it back. Why didn't I coun-
termand the order yesterday?

So I did.

No, I didn't.

This is an imposition, and I hate being imposed
upon. I tell her so, and she calls the proprietor,
who comes forward with a threatening demeanour.

He says he can't help it, if people don't know
their own minds, and go a-altering days.

I want to know what I'm to do with the dinner.
He wants to know what *he's* to do with it, and
matters become unpleasant.

Finally, I go home again with the dinner on my
hands, which isn't the proper place for it.

When I tell ROSE ANNA the pastrycook won't
take his things back, she says it serves me right.
This is a little hard on her part, I must say. I try
to make matters agreeable, and point out we
shall have enough to live upon for a month at
least.

ROSE ANNA says, " Stuff !"

I answer with one of my quiet smiles. "No, dear, we needn't stuff; moderation is best in all things." She doesn't see it.

We discuss what is to be done with the dinner. I suggest making it up into parcels and sending it to our disappointed guests of the previous day. ROSE ANNA pooh-poohs this idea.

By-and-bye, when the servant has gone to bed, ROSE ANNA wonders what that dish is with cream on the top. We go to see.

ROSE ANNA thinks it looks very good; she is also of opinion it would be a pity if it were spoiled; she wonders after that if it will spoil by keeping till to-morrow; she thinks we had better taste it, and see if it is quite good now.

She does so: it is good—very. She asks me to taste it. I had no notion till I took a spoon in my hand how hungry I was. Ultimately,—who proposed it I can't say,—we both sit down at the kitchen table, and make a capital supper.

ROSE ANNA recovers her temper and her spirits, and when I am inclined to lament over the bill I shall have to pay to the pastrycook, she becomes quite hilarious.

I go to bed, and have the nightmare!

CHAPTER IX.

ROSE ANNA wants some money.

I say, " How much ?"

She says, "Oh, a pound or two—five pounds will do—to pay the tradesmen and things."

I take a five-pound note from my little store, and, seeing how very little the store looks without it, begin to feel rather uncomfortable. On the knife-board of the omnibus, on my way to the office, I think things over, and feel more uncomfortable. I am the most uncomfortable of all, when, sitting at my desk, at COUTER AND PHLIMSY'S, I make a calculation on the office paper, and, trying to deduct thirty-five from twenty-one, in such a way that there shall be a remainder of fifteen, I find I can't do it.

The fact is, when we began housekeeping, ROSE

This is ROSE ANNA *waiting at the window for her husband's return from town of an evening. While thus employed,* MR. FULLALOVE *regrets to state that that rude young man opposite generally took the opportunity of kissing his hand to her.*

THIS IS AN ALLEGORICAL DESIGN,

Representing a perfect impossibility—i.e., a little unpleasantness during the very first week of the honeymoon.

ANNA'S mother and my mother gave us something for a start. ROSE ANNA is to have something every year. I also have something besides my office. At my office I have a rising salary. At present it is ninety pounds a year, and I rise five pounds annually—that is to say, if I show zeal.

The first thing of a morning it is, generally, my intention to show zeal, and I go on showing zeal up to about one o'clock, when I have lunch. After this I don't show as much zeal, and the head cashier and I usually have words.

To tell the truth, I'm not nearly as sure of that rise as I might be.

I calculate all day, and the head cashier makes himself very unpleasant. When I get home at night, the first thing I say to ROSE ANNA is—

"I want to say a few words to you, my dear, seriously."

She says, "Won't you have dinner first?" I don't see why not, and so I defer the revelation. Presently, however, I tell her, things can't go on as they are. We must be reasonable. We must turn over a new leaf.

Without waiting for an explanation, ROSE ANNA bursts out crying. I endeavour to explain through her sobs, but it makes her worse. I get pen, ink, and paper; and, referring to the trades-men's books, make a calculation

I am paralyzed at the result. ROSE ANNA is in the same condition. I smite my brow, and say we are ruined—in a hollow tone.

Upon continuing my calculations, I find I have made a slight error, and that we don't owe half as much as I first supposed. I hardly like to mention this to ROSE ANNA; it looks so stupid. However, perhaps, it will be best; for she may find it out afterwards.

When she hears the truth, she says, " It's all right then ; put away the nasty books, and don't let's bother any more." I endeavour to explain that it is anything but right, and I go on calculating all the evening, ROSE ANNA interrupting me at intervals by wishing she was dead.

In fact, we are so miserable at supper-time, we think we had better send out for a nice rump-steak and a bottle of sherry

When I come home next day, ROSE ANNA meets me on the door-step. She is joyous. She says, " Look at my dress !" I say, " Very nice !" She says, " It is a plain stuff thing I have bought to save my others. We really must economize."

I say, " How much was it, dear ?"

Instead of pursuing the subject further, ROSE ANNA takes me into the drawing-room, and points triumphantly to a row of plants in the window.

" What do you think I gave for them ?" she

asks. I must confess I feel annoyed. "Really, ROSE ANNA, I begin to think this extravagance—" "There, there," she replies, "I gave nothing." "Then they are cheap," I observe, in my sarcastic way.

I have a look at them. Three very crooked geraniums and a lop-sided fuchsia. They certainly are not worth much, and I am going to tell ROSE ANNA so, when she catches me round the neck, and exclaims, gushingly, "How do you think I got them, you old cross thing? You know that old great-coat of yours, and those old light trousers, and those old waistcoats that you talked about having done up? Well, when I came to look at them, they really weren't worth it. And such a nice respectful man came by with some flowers, and I knew you wanted some, but that we had no money to spend——"

"Do you mean to say you gave away all those clothes for this rubbish?"

"I should think not ; I have got two other pots —double pansies !"

From the first I see there is something wrong about the geraniums. Before a week is over the flowers fall off, and the stems grow pappy. I give one plant a tug, and find it has no root. It was probably planted the same day ROSE ANNA got it.

But I anticipate.

*　　　*　　　*　　　*　　　*

Upon the evening of the day we begin economizing, I send Rose Anna and the girl out to do some marketing.

I am certain things are much cheaper in the High Road than they are at our tradespeople's. Rose Anna says she would always prefer to do her own marketing, but somehow she never has a moment to herself.

"Now," she says, "do you think you can take care of the house while we are gone?"

"Of course I can," I reply; "why not?" But I hope there won't be much ringing at the bell.

There is a good deal of ringing. The man comes with the beer, and wants me to look whether we have got any of his pots. I say, "Come to-morrow."

A boy comes with some eggs, and I break one, taking them in. He laughs.

Then the washerwoman comes, bringing home the washing, and wants back the basket. I say, "Come to-morrow." About five minutes after she has gone, a little girl rings the bell and says, "Oh, please, sir, mother made a mistake, and left the wrong things. These belong to number six; I'll take them there, and bring yours back in a minute."

But she does not come back, and when ROSE ANNA returns home, I describe what has happened. She says, " How could you be so stupid !" and it presently appears that the little girl was a robber, and our clothes have been stolen. " Here's economy !" says ROSE ANNA.

* * * * *

One of the fellows at our place says to me one day, " Why don't you join our Society ?"

I say, " What Society ?" He says, " THE PROVIDENT CLERKS' FRIENDLY CO-OPERATIVE AND SELF-ASSISTING." I say, " What's the point of it ?" He answers, " It's first-rate." " In that case," I say, " I don't see why I shouldn't make one." " All right," he says, " tip us up your five shillings."

It seems that there is an entrance fee to this amount, and a half-crown annual subscription, which payments, as far as I can understand the rules, entitle you to the right of purchasing everything you want at half-price.

I say right off, " This is capital !" and I study the price list all the rest of the afternoon, under cover of one of COUTER AND PHLIMSY'S large ledgers.

When the office closes, I go to the Store, intent on making a purchase. Of course you know COU-

TER AND PHLIMSY'S is in the STRAND, close to
CHARING CROSS. The P.C. F.C. & S.A. Store is on
TOWER HILL. This is, I point out to the fellow
who got the five shillings out of me, rather inconvenient.

He says, "Why, there are heaps of omnibuses."
I take one, and thus start with an outlay of fourpence. If this sort of thing goes on, it will rather
cut into the profits.

When I reach TOWER HILL, I find, by all that
is provoking, I have left the half-sovereign I had in
the pocket of my office waistcoat. I have only a
shilling with me, and if I spend it all I shall have
to walk home.

This is horribly absurd, and I don't like to be
overcome by trifles. Certainly, the walk to HIGH-
LOW Terrace is not a trifle; it is about six
miles.

However, I won't be daunted, and enter the
Store. The question is, what can I get for a
shilling that is any use to me? Ah, a box of
Sardines! I consult my price list. Tenpence! I
take the change, and a penny boat from LONDON
BRIDGE to CHARING CROSS, where I mean to call
on POPKINS, who lives near our BANK, and borrow
my omnibus fare of him.

On the way I make a calculation: Sardines,
tenpence. Price at ordinary shop, one-and-three-

pence. Clear saving of fivepence. Deduct omnibus fare, fourpence, and penny boat. So far, anyhow, I'm not out of pocket.

I find my friend at tea, and ask him, in a joking
way, for the loan of a shilling. He gives it me, but
says—

"You're in no hurry: have a cup with me.
What's that parcel you've got? Sardines, by Jove!
well, that *is* lucky!"

I don't exactly see how I can refuse to give him
some, after he has lent me the shilling. Besides,
the things only cost tenpence. We open them, and
my friend eats two-thirds of the box with much
relish.

It is not unnatural, perhaps, that ROSE ANNA
should be a little out of temper, seeing how I have
kept the dinner waiting. I think it best not to
allude to the sardines, but ascribe the delay to the
tyranny of COUTER AND PHLIMSY.

The worst of it is, I don't feel very hungry, and
the meal (a pie of ROSE ANNA'S own making) is
difficult to swallow.

When dinner is done, I tell ROSE ANNA I have
got a surprise for her, and produce the price list.
She evidently has fancied I had brought her home
a present, and does not half enter into the point of
the thing, when I explain what it is.

I say, enthusiastically, "Look here, we can

live on half the money we do! I've joined a
Society where everything is to be had trade
price. For instance, what do you give for nut-
megs ?"

She doesn't know ; so I try moist sugar and the
best loaf. She is also vague upon these points.
Somehow, the " PROVIDENT CLERKS' FRIENDLY
CO-OPERATIVE AND SELF-ASSISTING " isn't cre-
ating half the effect it ought to do.

" Anyhow," I say, somewhat indignantly, " I
know everything's as cheap as dirt, and so you'll
find when you compare the prices with the trades-
men's bills." To add force to my statement, I also
observe, " You talked of a new silk dress, didn't
you ? Well, to-morrow I will take you to a place
where you can get one with fifty per cent. knocked
off."

ROSE ANNA seems not thoroughly to understand about the per centage, but her mind grasps
the other part of my statement, and she kisses me,
and calls me an angel, and puts extra milk and
sugar in my tea.

I get a half-holiday, next day, from COUTER
AND PHLIMSY'S, and we take a cab and go down
to the warehouse mentioned in the Provident
Clerks' circular.

It is a large building in a bye-lane in the City,
and we are jostled by porters carrying bales of

goods as we enter. There seems to be a great deal doing, and what is done appears to be on a gigantic scale. While we are waiting a man in front of us appears to be buying several miles of black velvet as coolly as I would buy a penny bun.

We wait a good bit, to tell the truth, and the warehousemen don't seem much impressed by us. Presently, however, I attract the attention of one of them, and ask to look at some black silks. He says, "This way," and, taking us to a counter, bangs down several tons in front of us. He evidently thinks we want a waggon-load, and I begin to grow nervous.

I therefore produce the little ticket I bought for my five shillings, and explain that I am a Provident Friendly "Oh," he says, in an injured tone, as though he had found out that instead of wanting to buy something, I had come in to sell matches.

Then he puts his hands in his pockets and calls to another warehouseman.

"Co-op," he says, and the other responds, "All right, Osess S," which extraordinary remark a knowing friend tells me afterwards is the slang for "last season's goods."

Presently we are served, and when ROSE ANNA has made her selection, which she does with a dissatisfied expression of countenance, we take away our parcel, and I breathe more freely in the cab. "And I don't believe the things are so cheap after all," says ROSE ANNA; "but the fact is, you spoilt it all by showing your ticket."

I have been wanting a new hat this ever so long, and I don't see why I should not get one. I again consult my circular, and we drive to the shop, and go in to make the purchase.

This time, though, I am more knowing, I ask to see one of their best hats, and the shopman offers ROSE ANNA a chair, and overwhelms me with attentions. When I am suited, I order my old hat to be done up and sent home, and produce a sovereign and the ticket.

At sight of the latter the shopman looks very blue indeed, and I fancy he, for a moment, has some idea of closing with me and recovering his property by violence. But he refunds the per centage like a lamb, and I depart in triumph.

Then ROSE ANNA and I have a nice little bit of dinner somewhere, and as we're in town, we think we may as well go to the play.

All things considered, without counting the cab, or the dinner, or the theatre, which, of course, were unnecessary expenses, we got the silk dress and the hat on reasonable terms.

Two days afterwards my old hat comes home, and ROSE ANNA says, "The man charged four-and-sixpence for doing it up."

"You never paid it ?" I say.

"Of course I did," says ROSE ANNA, "you never said I wasn't to."

CHAPTER X.

WE GO TO THE PLAY.

POPKINS has just been raffling some tickets for the theatre. The chances were a shilling each, and I have won four admissions to the boxes.

The tickets are for to-morrow, and I eagerly refer to the newspaper to see what is being played. POPKINS says it is a standard comedy. He also observes that if I want a good seat I had better mention the name of the gentleman who gave him the tickets. It is a gentleman connected with the suburban press, it appears; indeed, no other than WAVERLEY JONES, of the *Peckham Patriot*.

"An extraordinary character," POPKINS tells me, "awfully clever, and always drunk. Best talker you ever met in your life. Sleeps in his boots, and has done so for years."

This is ROSE ANNA *looking in at the little window in the door while she is yet labouring under the delusion that our ticket admits us to the Dress Circle. When presently she discovers that we have only got "Upper Boxes."* * * * *

The rest is too terrible for illustration.

When I am out at lunch, I mention these circumstances to a friend of mine, saying, in my off-hand way, "Got some tickets for the theatre from a literary friend—WAVERLEY JONES—you know."

My friend says, "*I don't* know. Who *is* WAVERLEY JONES?" This is a poser. But I get out of it rather cleverly, considering, and reply, "Oh, JONES that does all those clever things, you know, in the papers."

My friend says, "What clever things?" but just at this moment, I notice that my luncheon hour is up, so I have not time to pursue the subject.

*　　*　　*　　*　　*

ROSE ANNA has seen the tickets, and is in ecstasies. She says, "Who shall we take with us?"

There are some very nice girls in our terrace that I want ROSE ANNA to make acquaintance with—the JENKINSONS. I say, "Let's take two of the JENKINSON girls."

ROSE ANNA says, "I'm sure we shan't. Why, there's Aunty and Mamma."

I don't like to say, "Bother Aunty," and "Blow Mamma," because it would be ungentlemanly ; but such in my heart of hearts are my secret sentiments.

Without loss of time, ROSE ANNA sends a note

to her maternal parent, and to her other relative—
the same who came to see us—perhaps you may
remember. Next day, when I arrive at home, I
hear with joy that Mamma can't come, but am de-
pressed by the intelligence that Aunty's at liberty,
and is, at that moment, up stairs dressing.

When we are at tea (there is no time for dinner),
Aunty says, " As there was a fourth place, I took
the liberty of asking MR. BODGER ; I knew you
wouldn't mind. He'll meet us at the door, and
bring his opera-glass."

I'm not sorry to get BODGER'S glass, but I
don't see any necessity for BODGER. However, it
won't do to offend Aunty ; though, I must say, I
think it is a great liberty she has taken.

We are, it seems to me, an enormous length of
time over our tea, and I begin to think Aunty will
never leave off having another cup ; but she says
she enjoys it so. When the meal is over, she
" tittivates" before the chimney-glass, and I go for
a cab.

She is still tittivating when I come back again,
and I am nearly driven frantic by the slowness of
her movements, for by the kitchen clock it is already
a quarter past six, and the doors are open at half-
past. In a frenzied state I watch her pottering
with a tippet, and arranging and rearranging some
miserable ribbon ends in her cap.

But, at last, she is ready, and we are in the cab. I tell the man to drive his fastest. This is not very fast, but he does his best.

Presently, however, I see a public-house clock. "Hallo! Hang it all! that beast of an eight-day of ours!" *And now we have reached the theatre door twenty-five minutes before the time of opening!*

The people standing at the pit door, and the persons selling bills and oranges, are much amused, and look in at us through the window as though we were curiosities in a glass case.

MR. BODGER has not yet made his appearance. Aunty, in a cutting way, says, "He'll be here at the proper time;" and after a pause, observes, "I suppose the tickets are all right?"

I do not condescend to enter into any argument, but feel in my pocket.

I feel in another pocket; in a third, and a fourth; and then feel all over them again. I grow hot and cold, and my fingers shake so, the things fall from them and roll about the bottom of the cab.

Aunty and ROSE ANNA inquire the cause of my agitation, and there is no help for it but to tell them *I have left the tickets at home!*

We have some more excited talk upon this, and ROSE ANNA is for our giving up the affair altogether.   Aunty is for my paying for four admissions.   I take a middle course, and, leaving the ladies to wait for me, call a Hansom, and bid the driver go at full gallop to HIGHLOW TERRACE.

On the way I again examine my pockets, and, to my utter amazement, find that the tickets, after all, are in the corner of one.   Upon this I return triumphant : but, in the meantime, their cab has disappeared.

I send away the Hansom, and wait with what patience I can muster.   The persons with the play-bills and oranges attack me with much ferocity, and I buy a bill at last to keep them quiet.   But they are not quiet, as they want me also to buy an orange.

While I am waiting, the doors open, and it seems to me there is a dreadful rush.   The idea of a front seat I have abandoned some time ago.

What on earth has become of ROSE ANNA and Aunty ?

I supposed at first they were driving about to get through the time, but now they should be back again.   And where is BODGER ?

I don't know BODGER personally, and ask some one I see hanging about whether that is his name. He scowls at me and makes no answer.   All things considered, perhaps it is lucky he did not knock me down.

But the time goes on. This is maddening.

Have they gone home again ? Have they——
Oh, here they are.

I open the cab door with suppressed wrath. I say, "Well," in an impressive tone ; but they don't seem to notice it. I add, "You've done it this time, I must say ; all the places will be occupied."

"Oh, no!" says Aunty briskly ; and we enter the theatre. But here there is more misery in store for us. At the pay place I present the tickets, and am referred to another pigeon-hole. I present them there, and the man says, "You're too late ; you should have come before seven."

But at this moment an astonishing event occurs. Looking round, I see POPKINS. I tell my tale, and ask what is to be done? He says, "I'll manage it;" and takes the tickets back to the man at the pigeon-hole, and says something to him in a mysterious tone.

I overhear a part of it ; and, as far as I can understand, he is making me out to be the Editor of the *Times*. I feel more certain of a seat, but far from comfortable. Suppose the Editor of the *Times* should be here already, I should most likely get kicked out !

Whatever he says, however, we are passed through the wicket. We go up stairs, and a box-opener asks how many there are of us. I ask him whether he has any front places, and in return he inquires whether I want a bill. As I have one already, I say no. But he mistakes my meaning. He thinks I don't want to give him anything ; and, closing a door he has just opened, takes us round to the side, and shows us our seats. They are in the back row, and mine is behind a pillar.

When we are seated, ROSE ANNA says, "Why, these are the upper boxes, and the people have all got their bonnets on."

Upon investigation, I find that this is the case, which is annoying, as ROSE ANNA is in a low dress, and Aunty in a splendid cap with bright ribbons.

BODGER gets out his glass, but it does not enable him to see through the head of the person blocking out the view just in front of him. Then Aunty asks for the bill. I can't see anything myself, but it appears that ROSE ANNA and Aunty are not seeing the standard comedy mentioned on my bill, because there has been a change in the performance, only recorded on the bills sold within the theatre.

But they don't find this out for a long time, and are much puzzled.

Altogether it is not a successful evening, and I really think the least BODGER could have done, as he came home with us and ate an enormous supper, was to pay a portion of the cab fare.

He still lives opposite; he still stares at ROSA ANNA, *and annoys me more than ever.*

The above chaste and elegant design represents the memorable MAN-
TOWLER, ROSA ANNA'S *dear friend* FANNY—*till they quarrelled.*

CHAPTER XI.

WE HAVE A VISIT FROM ROSE ANNA'S DEAR FRIEND FANNY.

THE worst has come at last! Here is MRS. MANTOWLER!

You know by this time that we are, as it were, only in a small way of business in HIGHLOW Terrace. Our cot is lowly, but we are happy. At least we have been so, with few exceptions, up to this moment.

For all our little tiffs from time to time, ROSE ANNA and I adore one another,—or, anyhow, have been adoring one another until to-day. But MRS. MANTOWLER has come!

I find her in our little parlour when I come home in the evening. She is a monstrously fine creature, and fills our small apartment to overflowing. I thank Heaven that crinolines are gone out, when I see what an enormous space she contrives to occupy without one.

She is young, and beautiful, and bouncing. Aunty is bouncing also ; but this is a different sort of bounce—less heavy, and more effective.

She is sumptuously attired, and fragrant with a choice and insidious perfume, and she has manners which are at once elegant and overwhelming.

I have, somehow, fallen into an undignified way of entering my house by the back door. It is because we have lately been so unsettled with respect to servants, that, as a general rule, nobody takes any notice of me when I ring the visitors' bell. On this occasion I come in quietly at the back. The young person washing dishes says nothing about our having a visitor. I am a little untidy about some things, and I keep my bootjack in the kitchen, and my slippers in the parlour. I take my boots off, therefore, and, dreaming not of what I shall find there, enter the sitting-room in my stocking-feet.

I find ROSE ANNA has her best frock on, and the two ladies are reclining gracefully in easy chairs. ROSE ANNA introduces me to her friend :

"MR. FULLALOVE, my husband ; MRS. MAN-TOWLER—FANNY DASHINGTON that was, my dear —my old schoolfellow you have so often heard me talk about."

I bow, and smile. I have told you before that our parlour is not of large dimensions. My first impulse is to hide my feet beneath the table. I see, in the far distance, one of my slippers sticking out from round the sideboard, and I wonder whether they are both there, and, if so, whether presently, unobserved, I may obtain possession of them.

"FANNY is so kind as to say she will stop with us for a day or two," says ROSE ANNA.

I intimate that it is very kind of MRS. MAN-TOWLER; and I wonder when she is going to take her eyes off me, and whether my hair is very rough, and whether I, by chance, happen to have a smut on my nose.

It occurs to me afterwards, that I ought to have been brilliant and sparkling just about this period of our acquaintance, and then the beauteous FANNY might have been favourably impressed by me. Some time afterwards I can think of several sparkling things which I might have said if they had occurred to me at the moment.

But they didn't.

MRS. MANTOWLER waits for them, it seems to me. Finding they do not come, she addresses her conversation to ROSE ANNA.

Their conversation appears to me rather frivolous, and relates chiefly to persons I have never heard of, but I sit and smile.

I also cast sidelong glances towards the slipper.

As I sit there I ask myself why I don't say

something ; and why on earth I weakly sat down instead of immediately beating a retreat ?

The question is, how am I, now, to make my escape from the room ? Surely there can be no difficulty about doing this, in my own house too. It only wants a light *dégagé* air, and a trifling excuse. Qy. What shall it be ?

I surely cannot have been many moments hesitating. However, it is, now, too late. The servant-girl throws open the door, and announces dinner.

ROSE ANNA says,—

"My dear, will you take in MRS. MANTOWLER ?"

The moment has arrived ; I am speechless. She has caught sight of my stockings, and is evidently struck dumb with amazement.

What can she think ? I ask myself. It was bad enough to come into the room at first without my boots, but that is nothing to my idiotic behaviour in sitting there without them.

Under the circumstances, however, I think it best not to notice the fact. I therefore conduct MRS. MANTOWLER to the dining-room, and, having placed her in a seat, rush wildly back to the kitchen and struggle with my boots.

I get the right boot on the wrong foot, and the wrong boot on the right, and get neither off again because I can't find the bootjack.

Rose Anna calls to me while I am still struggling. My collar comes unbuttoned at the back, I burst a brace, but at length conquer my difficulties, and appear again in the dining-room.

I am a little out of breath, and rather confused. I say grace panting, and Rose Anna giggles. Mrs. Mantowler also is much amused. I look over at Rose Anna with an expression intended to apprise her that her mirth is ill-timed, but she says, laughing,—

"Do you know what you said?"

I coldly reply, "Grace."

She says, "Yes; but the one that ought to come afterwards."

I blush up a good deal at this; and the awkward part of it is, I don't exactly see how I can say the other, particularly after this levity, and I begin to serve the Julienne.

I have heard the expression among my fast friends—I don't think they are *very* fast, by the way—of a splash of soup. On this occasion it is literally so, and mostly over the side of the plate and on the cloth.

Rose Anna says, in a pet, "How clumsy!"

Mrs. Mantowler seeks to excuse me. She says—

"Don't be angry with him. He's only a little shy."

I don't like this sort of thing, but can't think of any felicitous rejoinder.

I therefore take my soup in silence, and pretend to be absorbed by the occupation. Presently it occurs to me that this is rather piggish, and I drop my spoon in confusion, when I find that the ladies have finished long ago, and are waiting for me.

While we are waiting for the meat, I notice that my struggles with those brutal boots have made my hands very dirty. I observe that MRS. MAN-TOWLER has also noticed the fact, and I get them, in my *dégagé* style, to the edge of the table, and hide them precipitately in my lap.

The roast fowl has come on now, and while I carve it I try to think of something to say.

I am on the point of thinking of something which will just do, when ROSE ANNA interrupts me by suggesting that I have got the knife in the wrong place in the bird.

I put the knife in another place, and get a limb off somehow. It is a wing, which FANNY has chosen. She particularized the liver-wing, and I hope to goodness she has got what she asked for. Anyhow, she makes no complaint.

Meanwhile the ladies converse with much liveliness, and I go on with my dinner. But this is getting awfully ridiculous.

Presently MRS. MANTOWLER says, "Is your husband always so silent?"

I blush tremendously at this, and ROSE ANNA answers, "He doesn't talk much — do you, dear?"

Upon this MRS. MANTOWLER observes, "He thinks the more, perhaps?"

A deadly hatred for MANTOWLER is rising within my breast.

"No, I don't," I reply, savagely; and she laughs, and says, "Don't you do either, then, MR. FULLALOVE?"

After this how can I talk to them, and what about? I feel that upon many subjects I could be brilliant, or at any rate diffuse; but this is not the time; and I fume in silence, feeling horribly ridiculous.

It is an enormous relief when at length the hateful meal, during which I hardly speak a hundred words, reaches its conclusion, and I am left to my wine.

I glare at my wine when I find it thus in my power. I gulp it in brimming bumpers. I have a sort of wild desire to carouse, to push around the bowl, metaphorically, and, all by myself, to lustily troll forth a Bacchanalian chorus.

But a glass or two too much always makes me so poorly afterwards, and I refrain.

Rose Anna opens the door, and says, "How can you be so absurd?"

"What do you mean?" I ask.

"What do *you* mean?" she retorts; and when she has gone away again I really don't know that I can satisfactorily answer the question.

To tell the truth, I rather fancy I have been making an idiot of myself.

But it must not go on. I take another glass, and go and wash my hands and brush my hair, in a little sanctum sanctorum I have got next to the back kitchen.

Then I put on a smiling countenance, and advance briskly towards the drawing-room. But when I am half way there the street door closes with a bang.

I look out of the window. My wife and her friend have left the house together.

I glance at the table, where a letter is lying, and find it addressed to me. Breaking it open I read these words,—

"Dear old Crosspatch,

"We have gone out to spend the evening, and hope you'll soon recover from your bad temper.

"Yours,

"Rose Anna and Fanny"

What does this mean?

Am I to calmly submit to this sort of thing?

If I am not, though, how am I to help it?

After all, what harm is there in my wife and her old schoolfellow going out together to spend the evening?

Certainly, they might as well have said where they were going to ; also, perhaps they might have asked me to accompany them.

But then, I must allow, that is a matter of opinion.

I think this, standing by the window and gazing pensively out upon the houses on the other side of the way, and whilst thus employed I am the witness of a remarkable occurrence.

You may remember a profligate person with an eye-glass who lived opposite, and who annoyed me a good deal some time ago by staring at ROSE ANNA?

He still lives opposite; he still stares at ROSE ANNA ; and he annoys me a good deal more than ever.

I have thought over this person's conduct more than once, and the more I think of it, the more I am disgusted ; but not being a fighting man, and he being very much so, I don't exactly see my way, with a whole skin, out of the difficulty.

6

At this identical moment I see him at his window, kissing his hand and telegraphing eagerly to some person in the direction which ROSE ANNA and FANNY have taken.

Is it for ROSE ANNA that these signs are intended ?

I am certain that he sees me looking at him, but he treats me with contempt, and continues to nod his head and smile. At this my blood begins to boil, and I rush to the door.

The ladies are not visible, but, looking across at that fellow's window, I see he has put his hat on, and a minute afterwards he comes down into the street, and passes me with a significant smile, taking the direction in which my wife went a few moments ago.

What does this mean ?

I ask myself the question in so awful a tone that it almost startles me in the gathering twilight.

As well as I am able to judge, without exactly knowing whether I shouldn't feel the same if I wasn't, I feel as though I were hovering upon the eve of a fearful discovery.

Under this impression my knees seem to give way under me, but I have yet sufficient strength to reach my hat off the peg, and follow in pursuit.

In the distance I observe the retreating form of the Destroyer of Domestic Happiness. He turns his head, and, seeming to observe me, quickens his pace.

I was not, then, deceived. He is following them. And what was the meaning of those signals? There is, undoubtedly, an assignation. But let them beware!

I am not precisely clear as to what they are to beware of, or what I shall say or do if I find that my suspicions are well founded.

I have a vaguely formed notion of appearing suddenly, and overwhelming them with my wrath. In the meantime the scoundrel's legs are so long that I am out of breath, and yet can hardly keep him in sight.

I don't know whether I have mentioned it before, but HIGHLOW Terrace is part of a horrible new neighbourhood, made up entirely of paltry little streets full of twopenny-halfpenny houses.

In pursuing the Destroyer, I have many opportunities of noticing the shortness of the streets, for he is everlastingly turning a corner, on which occasions I break out into a run, as I have seen the outside ones of a column of Volunteers do sometimes when they have been, what I think they call, right about wheeling.

G—2

Coming round one of these corners rather sharply, I find myself unexpectedly face to face with the Destroyer, who has had the meanness thus to lie in wait for me.

I am confused by this occurrence, and unable at the moment to put on an appearance of wanting to go anywhere in particular.

He asks me, in his impudent way, whether I want him.

I say, no, I don't want him.

He says, " All right, then."

After this I walk on, and am not sorry to turn the next corner. But I am not going to tamely submit to be beaten in this way. Though if I don't, what am I to do?

I feel, in the first place, that it is necessary that I should dissemble, and I begin practising it round the corner. I also endeavour to call to mind what the last of the Mohicans was in the habit of doing when following in the trail of the wily Chingachgook. But my reminiscences do not assist me.

After a time, I feel that I have dissembled long enough where I am, and peep round the corner.

The Destroyer, it appears, is dissembling round another corner at the end of the street, and pokes his head out at the same moment that I thrust forth mine, and we catch one another, and jerk back.

In jerking back my head, I bump it. I hope he has done the same.

Shortly after—when I have done rubbing, I think it is time to peep again. I peep for some time and see nothing. I venture forth and reconnoitre with the same result.

He has escaped!

But no! In the distance I again catch sight of him walking quickly away. Again I follow, but with renewed caution.

It is almost dark now, and I have some difficulty in keeping him in sight; but yet I feel convinced he knows I am still following.

Presently he reaches a cab-stand; here he pauses for a moment and glances round, then plunges into one of the vehicles.

It is a certainty now! But my mind is made up.

I see him depart in one four-wheeler. I then call another.

I say to the driver, " Follow that cab !"

He does so, as it seems to me, at a gallop, and begins calling out to the other cabman to stop.

I roar out to my man to leave off. The other cabman pulls up, and wants to know what my man wants.

My man says he understood the gent inside wanted to speak to him.

At this I slip down into the bottom of the vehicle and grovel on all-fours in abject terror.

While I am among the straw, I hear the other driver calling out to me, and he says,—

"What's come to 'im, BILL? I think he's took poorly."

I am rather pleased when the other cab goes on again, and I have a little talk with my driver.

I candidly tell him that he is a bungling idiot, and he touches his hat. I add, with the same straightforward frankness, that he is a dolt, and a dunderhead, and he nods at me and winks his eye with intense meaning.

There is no doubt about him. He is all I have said, and also a little deaf.

In the meanwhile we are following the other cab. We are going a long way. What will the fare be, I wonder? But this is not a moment to think of such trifles.

It will be the moment, though, presently.

The other cab has stopped at last. What is this? A public-house. It has stopped for beer.

I should like some myself, but I must remain in concealment. I see the Destroyer enter the tavern, and see him come back again wiping his mouth, and again we pursue our wild career.

After a time we, once more, come to a stand-

still. Where are we now? The HOLBORN
CASINO!

This is too awful! He has gone in. I alight,
pay my fare, and ask myself what is to be done
next? It is not possible that I, a respectable married man, can go into such a place. Besides, it is
impossible that ROSE ANNA——

I am interrupted here by a violent blow on the
back. It is that fellow POPKINS who has struck
me.

"Hallo, FONDLING!" he says, using a nickname
they gave me at the bank; "you're not a-going it
at all, I don't think. Won't I just tell Mrs. F"

I repudiate this libertine suggestion, and ask
him how he dares?

He says, "Don't talk nonsense, old fellow.
Come in."

He pulls me towards the entrance, but I shake
myself free with virtuous indignation; and laughing, he calls me an old slyboots, and leaves me
outside.

* * * * *

I have been waiting two hours. The Destroyer
has not yet reappeared, and nothing remarkable has
happened.

* * * * *

I have waited three hours. The gas is being put out. The votaries of the light fantastic are separating. The Destroyer comes out at last, and departs also.

I have seen nothing to warrant my suspicions. An impression is upon my mind that in this instance I have acted rather absurdly.

* * * * *

It has come on to rain. It rains faster. I find I have not money for a cab. I turn up my coat-collar.

* * * * *

I am at home at last. I am soaked to the skin. I see a light in the parlour. I knock ferociously, and ROSE ANNA comes to let me in with a yawn. " What on earth have you been doing ?" she says.

" What have *you* been doing ?" I retort.

" Waiting for you ever since half-past six."

" You did not go out, then, to spend the evening ?"

" Of course not. It was only our fun."

I like fun !

Immediately there is a loud pop, and a tall and fearful flame shoots up.

This is ROSE ANNA *waiting for the fire engine. Want of space only prevents the introduction in the above illustration of the engine in question, accompanied by the beadle of the parish, and thirteen and a half small boys, (the half had two wooden legs.)*

CHAPTER XII.

WE ARE BLOWN UP.

WE are in a bad way in HIGHLOW Terrace—
in a very bad way generally—but in particular in a very bad way for gas.

It is given to going out suddenly, and without
any sort of warning. Then, coming on again, still
more suddenly, with a smell.

It always wants water in its metre or its pipes.
It sings like a tea-kettle. We have had our bedroom floor up twice already, to do something to it,
and it has given a worse light each time, after the
something has been done.

We also live in continual dread of explosions.
ROSE ANNA is given to nervous attacks, and they
generally take the direction of gas. I think ROSE
ANNA and I have had more unpleasantness upon
this subject than any other.

see us, we were left in total darkness, and that she thought it was what she kindly called, " One of my monkey tricks ?"

Did I tell you that in doing something with a hammer and nail—I have a weakness for hammers and nails, only I generally knock in the latter a little askew—did I tell you that I made a hole in the gas-pipe by driving a nail into it, and that we were nearly blown up by the gas, and unmistakably so by the landlord ? Also, that I had to pay a good sum for the gas that escaped ?

Did I tell you that after MARIA got warning she used to break a lamp-globe every day regularly ? Oh, you little know what we young housekeepers have to put up with !

We did have an explosion yesterday, but it did not do much mischief, except shaking us a little, frightening ROSE ANNA into hysterics, and spoiling our dinner. When she is restored to convalescence, she abuses the gas, and refuses to allow it in the house.

I say mildly, " Turn it out, my dear!" This is one of my sharp things, but she becomes very angry, and, regarding me with an appalling expression, wishes to know whether I can do nothing better than joke, when we've all been nearly blown into the adjacent brickfield ?

I wish to conciliate her, and promise to bring

home a lamp next day. I do bring home a lamp, and deposit it upon the table, with one of my knowing smiles.

ROSE ANNA objects before I take the paper off it. She says it is too small ; that it is not the right sort ; that she wonders who's going to trim it, for she isn't, and the servant can't.

I explain to her how simple the operation is, with the air of a scientific lecturer. Indeed, I humorously burlesque the style of Professor POLY-TECHNIC, but she doesn't seem to see the point.

I prepare to illustrate my lecture by experiments. I turn up the wick, and hold a match to it.

Immediately there is a loud pop, and a tall and fearful flame shoots up.

ROSE ANNA screams. I am a little flustered myself. I twist the machinery in the wrong direction, then twist it back violently. Eventually I turn down the wick, burning my fingers severely in so doing.

Instead of the flame there is now a column of black smoke, and smuts fall in every direction as thick as blackberries. I may mention that there is also an odour !

ROSE ANNA, as usual, unreasonable, cries, " Take the horrid thing away !"

I try to remonstrate, but she is obstinate.

She is all over blacks, and presents a mottled and unnatural appearance. I look at myself in the glass. I am like a half-washed Christy's Minstrel.

I put the best face I can on it. I say it will be all right presently, and I twist the machinery up and down, hoping it may. Somehow, at last it is. I have not the remotest notion why, but it is burning properly at last ; and even ROSE ANNA—who, I must say, is about one of the most wrong-headed women that ever lived—is forced to admit it is a good light. But when she sees her beautiful carpet speckled and spoilt, she scowls through the smoke.

To reassure her, I explain to her that the stuff we burn in the lamp is non-explosive. She says she doesn't care, and she won't stop in the room to be covered with smuts by her husband, who ought to know better.

Firmly, but mildly, I request her to remain, if not from inclination or obedience, at all events for the love of science.

I pour some of the oily spirit into a plate, and plant myself in an attitude, as I say, quoting the language of the shopkeeper's printed bill, and extending a whisp of lighted paper over the plate,—

"The oil is perfectly harmless, and will not

catch fire, even if lighted paper be applied to it—
nor will it explode."

At this instant, however, a boy outside, passing
by the garden railings, cracks his whip, and ROSE
ANNA and I both jump back, terrified.

I recover myself, and implore her to be calm.
I also try to look as if I had not jumped myself.

Then I resume my experiments. I again apply
the paper. A ghastly blue flame hovers over the
plate. I am not sure what this means, but feel no
uneasiness, in consequence of what the shopman
has told me.

But, puff! The beastly stuff has suddenly
burst into flame! It rages with fury!

I throw away my lighted paper, which falls upon
the ornament in our fire-stove.

I try to blow out the burning oil, and only
blow it over the plate. It runs about the table
blazing.

I am, under these circumstances, naturally excited. I upset a few things, and break a few others,
but I can't extinguish the flames.

Of the two, perhaps, ROSE ANNA is the most
terrified. In order that the conflagration may have
full play, she has opened the window. She also
puts her head out, and screams, "Fire!"

That boy with the whip, and some other boys—
there are always any number of them, it seems to

me, hanging round our railings—respond vociferously. Before long the entire neighbourhood is ringing with the warning cry, and the Terrace is up in arms and out of window.

I have, however, no time to think of these matters. I see that the moment has arrived—indeed, I am not quite sure it has not passed—when everything depends on coolness and promptitude.

As calmly as I can, whilst the flames, so to speak, are raging round me, I pause to reflect upon the course which it is best to pursue.

The new hearth-rug suggests itself to me. I seize it, and upset the fender. Calm and resolute amidst the din, I devote myself to my task, and my exertions are crowned with success.

The fire is got under, and finally extinguished. As well as the smoke will allow me to do so, I breathe again.

Meanwhile, however, ROSE ANNA has been screaming out of window. Now that the hour of danger has passed, the absurdity of this conduct on her part strikes me forcibly.

I say to her, in my quiet way, " Don't make yourself ridiculous !"

She says, not noticing my sarcasm, " Thank goodness, it's coming !"

I say, " What ?" and as she makes no answer, look out of window.

I descry, in the far distance, a lanky fire-escape being propelled towards our house, while, by a shouting and cracking of whips, the sound of galloping steeds, the thunder of wheels, and the loud murmur of the juvenile populace, I have every reason to believe the parish engine is close at hand.

With that presence of mind of which I have in these chapters so frequently given instances, I at once see what must be done.

I secure the front door by means of bolt and chain, and resolutely plant my back against it.

*   *   *   *   *

The beadle and his myrmidons have entered by the other door in the rear of my premises.

*   *   *   *   *

We burn gas again now. Our pretty little drawing-room is quite spoilt, and our beer cask is empty. The beadle and his myrmidons were thirsty souls.

I believe, too, I shall be called upon to pay five pounds to-morrow.

And all this misery is owing to ROSE ANNA'S absurd objections to gas. I point the fact out to

her, not unkindly, and she flies into one of her
worst paroxysms.

The last thing I remember her to say before I
fall asleep is that she wishes she was at home again
with her mother.

"FOR BETTER, FOR WORSE."

This is on the whole rather a fanciful picture, but yet not as fanciful as at first you might suppose.

This is the MANTOWLER again—according to her own account— playing one of those celebrated matches of hers, of which we heard so much during the construction of our billiard room.

CHAPTER XIII.

WE GO IN FOR SPORTS AND PASTIMES.

" BUT, why not ?" says MRS. MANTOWLER.

"It wouldn't cost much," chimes in ROSE ANNA.

"It would be such an improvement," urges my wife's friend.

"You *must* do it !" says my wife, clinching the matter with much emphasis.

And all this came from a broken window!

ROSE ANNA, in one of her playful moods, threw a sofa-cushion at me, bless her dear little heart ! I returned it, missed her, and broke a pane of glass. "What great events from trivial causes spring !" as the poet truly observes.

We send for our landlord, who is a builder, carpenter, painter, and glazier, and what not ?

He says he will have it mended and stands

scratching his head. Presently he gives utterance to a grand idea.

The pane of glass broken is in a French window opening into our garden. He says, if he may make so bold, he would suggest a few more panes of glass, and making a little conservatory outside. ROSE ANNA clasps her hands, and says, "Lovely!" MRS. MANTOWLER smiles at me bewitchingly, and says, "Fairy-like!" I demur, and say, "Think of the expense!" ROSE ANNA bothers the expense, and MR. COMPO urges that there is one pane of glass to mend, anyhow, and it wouldn't cost much more while we are about it.

"We might pick our own oranges off our own trees!" says my wife.

"Grow your own camellias for your own hair, love!" says my wife's friend.

"Force vegetable marrers fust rate!" interjects MR. COMPO.

"We shall cut out the whole terrace!" exclaims the wife of my bosom, triumphantly.

"You'll never repent it!" puts in the landlord.

Three to one isn't fair. I daren't say no, and I don't want to say yes. I take my stand on the old ground of expense.

"No hurry about payment," says MR. COMPO.

"I'll soon save it out of the housekeeping!" declares ROSE ANNA, still smiling bewitchingly.

"I'll send you a pot of musk to start it," says MRS. MANTOWLER.

"No," I answer at last, summoning up all my resolution; "I can't afford it."

"Oo—o—h!" sobs ROSE ANNA, taking out her pocket-handkerchief, while her friend looks daggers at me.

"Did I marry and leave a comfortable home to be treated like this?" asks my wife. MRS. MAN-TOWLER thinks men are all brutes. MR. COMPO asserts some people are blind to their own interests. I may observe, I don't believe MR. COMPO is one of those people.

At last, after many tears and entreaties, I rashly consent to think about it, and take my departure for my bank, where I arrive late, as usual.

My head is running on conservatories all the day, and I make many mistakes in consequence, and sketch small Crystal Palaces all over my blotting paper.

I ask a friend his opinion on greenhouses. He thinks them stunning. I ask another, and he says "scrumptious."

I promised to think about it. I did think about it, and am still thinking when I reach HIGHLOW Terrace in the evening.

I find in front of my house, lying in the road, a heap of scaffold-poles, big enough for a cathedral, and numerous enough to form lances for a whole regiment of Brobdignagians. I also find an assortment of ladders, two or three loads of bricks, and a splodge of mortar : into this latter I put my foot. In olden times they would have called this an evil omen ; I called it a dirty mess. MR. COMPO is sitting on the top of the bricks, two men are leaning against them smoking pipes, three boys are playing at buttons alongside.

MR. COMPO touches his hat respectfully. He thought, he says, he might as well bring a few things in case I should decide on building the conservatory. I tell him I haven't decided yet, and go into the house. He follows me into the passage. ROSE ANNA and MRS. MANTOWLER rush out and seize me on either side, and drag me into the drawing-room.

They tell me to look, and I look. Pinned up against the wall, to the injury of the paper, are huge plans, all of which have the name of LORD STARVELING upon them at the top, while at bottom I read such inscriptions as " Front elevation," " Ground plan," &c., &c.

" What is the meaning of all this folly ?" I ask, sternly.

The two ladies, speaking both at once, inform me that MR. COMPO has just erected a conservatory for LORD STARVELING, and will put one up for me exactly similar, only a little smaller, for next to nothing.

Still I demur; but I am only human, and I say, with a magnanimous air, "ROSE ANNA, you shall have your conservatory, if I go through the court for it!"

She kisses me, and calls me a kind dear old man. MRS. MANTOWLER congratulates me; MR. COMPO grins approvingly; and I inspect the plans.

"Hullo!" I say, "what's this?"

"That, my dear," replies my wife, playfully, " is the billiard-room opening out of the conservatory."

I am thunderstruck.

"ROSE ANNA," I say, "there are limits to human forbearance, and there are bottoms to the deepest purses. Beware!"

ROSE ANNA wants to know what she has done to be spoken to in that way.

MR. COMPO says he knows I'm a gentleman, and won't go back after giving my word to a lady.

Oh dear, oh dear! I wish COMPO and that MANTOWLER, and bricks and mortar, and everything else, were at the bottom of the sea!

*　　　*　　　*　　　*　　　*

Oh, that accursed COMPO!

Oh, that billiard-room !

MRS. MANTOWLER, MRS. MANTOWLER ! you are the serpent that I have cherished ; and you, as it ever was, have turned and stung me. Is this your gratitude for all the good things you have eaten and wine you have drunk beneath my roof, showing itself now by urging me to beggary, bankruptcy, and suicide ?

Oh, ROSE ANNA ! ROSE ANNA, oh !

Not a moment's peace have I had since that fellow COMPO declared that LORD WHAT'S-HIS-NAME had a billiard-room opening out of his conservatory.

ROSE ANNA says she *will* have a billiard-room.

MRS. MANTOWLER says she shall have a billiard-room.

COMPO says she must have a billiard-room.

I don't see that it ever particularly matters what I say.

She'll be entering horses for the Derby next, I suppose. Where *is* the money to come from ? That's all I'm thinking of. And now both the women declare I gave my consent, and the foundations are dug, and COMPO has possession of the premises.

Where will it end ?

I hear nothing but billiard talk of an evening.

Cannons! Ugh! I'm not a volunteer. Kisses! I shudder at this reckless impropriety of expression. Pockets! One must have deep ones, well lined.

MRS. MANTOWLER says it's a beautiful game. ROSE ANNA says she could play day and night.

This is a pleasant prospect, by the way.

MRS. MANTOWLER buys sporting papers, and reads me the accounts of the great matches, how somebody made ninety-four off a break, and how somebody else scored fifteen red hazards consecutively.

I sit and listen to these wonders with an inward quaking. I daren't for the life of me say I don't understand the horrid jargon, for when MRS. MANTOWLER asked me whether I played billiards, I said, "Of course!" and gave her to understand I was rather a good hand at it.

If I recollect aright, I think I said, at the time, in my off-hand way, "I can play a pretty sure game."

I had heard the expression at COUTER AND PHLIMSY'S, and treasured it up.

I didn't think I was doomed to have a billiard-table when I made that statement. The truth is, I never had a cue in my hand but once in my life, and then I cut a hole in the cloth, and had to pay a guinea for the mending of it.

Now I am to have a billiard-table of my own, what *shall* I do with it? I shall look such a fool if I don't know what to do with it when I have got it.

I know what I'll do. I'll start out after dinner, and go to the public-house round the corner, where they've got a table, and watch the players attentively.

A good idea! I steal out. I go to the public-house round the corner, and make my way to the billiard-room.

Two gentlemen in their shirt-sleeves are playing. They have very black moustaches, very large watch-chains, huge rings on their fingers, and enormous cigars in their mouths.

They say, "Good evening, captain!" as I enter.

My manly bosom fills with pride. It has always been my opinion that my appearance had something of the martial in it, though ROSE ANNA was pleased to be sarcastic when I stated this opinion. But here are perfect strangers who take me for a military man.

The two gentlemen knock the balls about a good deal, but don't appear to do much. One of them, however, seems very sure of winning, for he wants to bet what they call odds, I think, that he does. The other whispers me to take him, as he can "wop him easy."

I shake my head in my knowing way, and say, "Wait a bit," and order a glass of grog and a big cigar of the marker. I am perfectly well aware that either taken by itself will make me ill, but I hope that the two combined will neutralize each other.

By-and-by, the game comes to an end. If I had betted, I should have won five-and-twenty shillings. What a fool I was!

"Have a game, captain?" says one of the moustachioed gentlemen.

I explain I don't know much about it. He offers to teach me. This is the chance for which I have been longing. I take off my coat, and choose a cue.

I choose a cue with some care, though I must confess I don't exactly know the good ones from the bad. When chosen, I chalk my cue, and I don't spare the chalk.

So far I feel that I am doing the correct thing, and now for the game itself.

My opponent says, "Will you break?" Break what? What does he want me to do? He who breaks pays. Does he want me to pay? I suppose that's it. I say,

"How much?"

He laughs and plays first. "Now, captain, go it!" he says. I go it, but don't do much good apparently, for he scores directly afterwards and I don't.

It seems to me that if I only hit hard enough I must do something. I "put my back into it,"— that's his expression, not mine—and two balls disappear into two pockets.

"Good shot! First-rate, by JOVE!" says my opponent's friend.

"Great stroke!" says the marker, putting six on to my score.

"Six to four I win," says my adversary.

"Take him," says the other; "he can't play a bit."

Where does he want me to take him to, I wonder? However, I say, "All right," and my adversary says, "Done with you, captain."

I lose that game. I have another glass of grog, and light my cigar for the sixth time. I bet. I win. I exult. "Marker, glasses round."

I play again. I win. Again. I lose. My cue wants chalking. More grog. I bet. I lose. Another light.

I lose again. One more glass. I play. I'm not quite sure whether I win or lose this time. We're all jolly good fellows! I'm a particularly jolly good fellow! "Let's have another glass."

Nothing like billiards, after all. MRS. MANTOWLER'S a brick. Bet six to four Mrs. MANTOW-

LER'S a brick. "What's to pay?" Won't go home till morning.

Finally the two gentlemen who have taught me billiards, conduct me to HIGHLOW Terrace. They prop me up against the door, then knock loudly and walk away.

ROSE ANNA answers knock (which is rather a loud one) with wrath on her brow. Somehow or other I fall down.

Somehow it does not seem worth while getting up again. I tell her I'm all right. She vanishes. I fancy I hear her weep, and MRS. MANTOWLER laugh somewhere in the distance. Bet six to four MRS. MANTOWLER'S a brick. I like women who laugh. I hate women who cry. ROSE ANNA'S always crying.

"Let's have another game."

*   *   *   *   *

It is next morning. I awake with a headache. ROSE ANNA reproaches me bitterly. She wants money for housekeeping. I feel in my waistcoat pocket, where last night I had three sovereigns and some loose silver. I find a fourpenny-piece and a bit of chalk. This is dreadful.

Billiard lessons are expensive.

CHAPTER XIV.

WE ARE VERY NEARLY MURDERED IN OUR BEDS.

I AM rather poorly.

I will not go so far as to say that I am positively ill, but it is one of those occasions when one feels one ought to go to bed early and have a nice basin of hot gruel.

From time immemorial the FULLALOVES have taken gruel in all cases of emergency. We are believers in gruel, and have been so for ages past—probably ever since gruel was first invented.

It is also the custom of the FULLALOVES to tallow their noses when suffering from cold in the head, as you may have seen the comic characters do in the pantomimes. The winding of a stocking round the throat in like cases has long been one of the institutions of our family; and there is a particular kind of pill which the FULLALOVES have

A NIGHT OF TERROR IN HIGHLOW TERRACE.

The above represents ROSE ANNA *listening for the thieves.* MR. FULLALOVE, *though invisible, is supposed to be assuming a warlike attitude on the landing below.*

I picture myself shooting the thieves. MRS. MANTOWLER *says,*
" Why don't you go down and see?"   Some women are so unreason
able '

always gone in for, and must have swallowed many
thousands of in their time.

I feel rather poorly, as I observed before, and I
retire to rest shortly after tea.

When interrogated by Rose Anna, it is possible
that I may, to some extent, exaggerate my ail-
ments. I do not know that it is positively necessary that I should groan; but I do so, and seem
to be relieved by it.

Rose Anna sympathizes with me, and makes
the gruel with her own hand. I almost wish she
had shown her sympathy another way; for it is
rather lumpy and a little smoked.

Mrs. Mantowler—she is really a great creature when one knows her—suggests brandy to
improve the flavour. Rose Anna says, "Yes, a
teaspoonful." Mrs. Mantowler says, "Fiddle-
stick!" and pours with a liberal hand.

I feel much better after this, and close my eyes
in gentle slumber. The ladies meanwhile amuse
themselves down stairs. Waking up some time
later, I hear the piano going, and Mrs.
Mantowler's voice singing in its loudest
key.

Rose Anna joins in the chorus.

What is it they say? They are walking in the
Zoo; they are nobody's children. And what is
this? They are chickaleary blokes, if my ears do

not deceive me, and Whitechapel is the village they were born in!

Wherever could MRS. MANTOWLER have picked up such extraordinary songs? MR. MANTOWLER must be a very strange person!

I wish there was less chorus to them, however; and I can't be mistaken—no! there is a smell of tobacco!

At my desire a rushlight has been left burning by the bedside. I consult my watch, and find, to my surprise, that it is past one o'clock. It seems to me that these festivities are somewhat heartless on ROSE ANNA'S part.

I have the strongest suspicion that MRS. MANTOWLER is smoking a cigar. I feel confident that there is a consumption of hot spirits and water upon the part of the ladies. If I hadn't made out I was so very poorly, I would certainly go down stairs and see what was going on. As it is, however, I close my eyes again. I also cover up my ears, and once more sink into repose.

*   *   *   *   *

The bedroom door flies open with a crash. ROSE ANNA and her friend are by the bedside. Their hair is in paper.

(MRS. MANTOWLER does not look so well under these circumstances.)

Their faces are white, and a bedroom candlestick in ROSE ANNA's hand trembles violently.

My first impression is, that it is cigars and brandy-and-water; but ROSE ANNA, in an agitated whisper, tells me it is thieves!

I am hardly awake yet, and am conscious of having been taken at a great disadvantage. The first law of nature, self-preservation, suggests seeking shelter beneath the bed-clothes, but second thoughts tell me that a more manly course will be to get up and do something.

In the first place, however, it will be as well to decide what.

I therefore ask ROSE ANNA to try and calm herself, and, if possible, to combine intelligibility with the process; in other words, to say, what has happened?

To this both ladies replying at once, in greater agitation than ever, inform me that there are robbers trying to break into the house; that some one has been shaking the back parlour window; that they (the ladies) feel certain we shall all be murdered in our beds.

There isn't anybody in bed but myself, for the servant is at the door, shivering, in her night-cap. However, it is certain that steps should be taken.

MRS. MANTOWLER says, with energy, "Haven't you a pistol or anything?"

I haven't a pistol or anything.   In fact it occurs to me, on reflection, that the deadliest weapon available is a handsaw in the back kitchen, and perhaps there mayn't be time to get it.

How can there be time, indeed?   The only wonder is, why the robber has not broken in before this, for, owing to the works in progress in the rear of our premises, a person wishing to come in has only got to step over the doorstep and do so.

Suddenly an idea occurs to me.

We have got a watchman's rattle.

I mention this fact to ROSE ANNA, and suggest that it shall be sprung.

She says, "Where is it?"

I reply, "How am I to know?"

She says, "You had it last."

I say, "That's like you."

But MRS. MANTOWLER very pertly remarks, that perhaps it would be as well to look for it, and quarrel at some more fitting opportunity.

Upon this we all set to looking for the rattle, and occasionally listen at the top of the stairs to hear if the robbers have broken in yet.

About half an hour thus elapses.   It seems to me that if the robbers *have* broken in, they will probably by this time have sacked the premises.

I mention this idea to MRS. MANTOWLER, and she says, "Why don't you go down and see?"

Some women are so unreasonable.

We have found the rattle at last, and I spring it vigorously out of window.

I succeed in awakening the whole terrace, but there are as yet no signs of a policeman.

This is certainly a nice state of things. People to be robbed and murdered in this way with perfect impunity!

MRS. MANTOWLER says, "There's been no bloodshed as yet."

I answer, "Whose fault is that?" and even at this moment I fancy I hear a heavy footfall below.

This is becoming horrible.

We are so much occupied in springing the rattle, we don't notice that there is some one calling to us from over the garden railings. It rather startles me when I do notice him at last.

It is a young man, who says, "What's up, guv'nor?"

I reply, briefly, "Burglars!" and go on with my rattle.

He says, "Where are they, sir?"

I say, "Down below."

He says, "Come down, and open the door, then."

I say, in my sarcastic style, " Not for Joseph !"
and he answers, coarsely, " Don't make a worse
idiot of yourself than you can help.   I'm a policeman in private clothes."

*   *   *   *   *

After all, there is no robber down stairs.   The
question is, has there been one ; and if so, what
has he taken ?   We look about, and find that
things are much as they were.   The oil-cloth is
still in the passage, and the wall-paper has not
been removed.

I may be slightly agitated, or the door-chain is
more obstinate than usual.   At any rate, I am a
long while getting the door open.   When I have
done so, and have let in the policeman in plain
clothes, I feel unaccountably relieved in my
mind.

He says, " Now, what's all this ?" and when I
have explained, proposes a tour of the premises.   I
take up a poker, and we make the tour.   We use
great caution in so doing, and, generally, lie in
wait, and pounce out, and dart in ; but we don't
catch anybody in particular, unless perhaps it is the
cat.

The scullery door sticks fast, and we make a
rush at it.   It resists our attack, and we make

another rush. Then it gives way rather unexpectedly, and we sprawl.

While sprawling, I instinctively defend myself with the poker. Some one closes with me. We are in the dark, and I can't see who is my antagonist, but he keeps a tight hold of my collar.

I am desperate, and keep a tight hold of his. We struggle madly—breathlessly. We bump each other's heads upon the floor. I cry out "Oh!" when my head is bumped, and my antagonist says, " Hallo ! who's that ?"

I say, " It is I ; are you the policeman ?"

He says, " Yes : why the dickens didn't you say who you were before ?"

I reply, with dignity, " This is trifling !" and we get up and strike a match. We then continue our search.

Eventually we find nobody, and the policeman in private clothes says he thinks he may as well go.

I agree with him.

He wishes to drink my health first, and does so in draughts of raw spirits. Then he says, " I will report this to the inspector, and he will call in the morning."

I say, " Very well."

ROSE ANNA and MRS. MANTOWLER come down stairs now that all danger is past, and suggest that the policeman shall have something to drink.

I say, " He has had some."

MRS. MANTOWLER says, "Give him some more?"

He agrees to this arrangement, and has a good lot more. I have a suspicion he was in liquor when he came. There can be no doubt about his being so now.

He tells us anecdotes, and I listen, yawning. However, the ladies seem amused.

I want to go to bed, and give him five shillings, hoping he will go. He only stops longer.

When the spirits are all gone, however, he takes his departure, and some time or other I am able to go to sleep again.

Next day, which is Sunday, a policeman calls. He examines the premises very carefully.

He intimates that the other policeman in plain clothes must have been an impostor. "Perhaps," he says, "he wanted to make a plan of the inside of your premises. He was probably a pal of the thieves."

This intelligence disturbs me.

I send for the inspector. We go deeper into the matter. We find footsteps in the garden. We measure them, and it seems that they will form a clue to the mystery. In the end they prove to be COMPO, the builder's, and don't form a clue.

I ask the inspector to put two or three extra

men on duty that night, and he promises he will.

I resolve to buy at least one revolver on Monday morning. I know a friend who has a sword-stick, and will borrow it. Then we shall be safe.

At least tolerably safe.

The night passes without much alarm. We retire early, and next morning nobody is found murdered in bed. There is nothing like taking precautions. The burglars see we are determined, and they quail.

On Monday night I bring home, with some ostentation, a revolver and a sword-stick. They object to the former inside the omnibus, and I have some trouble in explaining to the other eleven passengers that my intentions, as far as they are concerned, are harmless.

That night we load the deadly weapon. I trust we load it properly. No matter, we do load it.

We stop up a little later than usual, and have a glass of something hot after a hot supper. We sing songs. MRS. MANTOWLER sings all she knows of the "Chickaleary Bloke." As far as I am able, I join in the chorus.

Altogether we have a jolly evening, and when I go upstairs to bed, I somehow find I have forgotten to change my boots for my slippers.

I undress, and then open the door to put out my boots on the landing.   Horror !

A dreadful sight meets my eyes.   I rub my eyes—but no, I am not deceived.

I come back into the bed room for my revolver, and tell ROSE ANNA that there is a light downstairs in the parlour.

She rushes in to MRS. MANTOWLER, and we all peep over the head of the stairs.

Yes, there is a light.   The thieves are in the house.   What is to be done ?

We come down stairs on tiptoe, I clutching my revolver.   MRS. MANTOWLER and ROSE ANNA follow with the sword-stick.

After I have fired off my five barrels, if I hit no one, I can fall back on my other deadly weapon.

It is a thriiling moment.   I feel that our case is desperate.   We may be going to death, but we go all the same—resolutely.

The parlour door is ajar.   We peep in breathlessly.

I put the muzzle of the revolver round the corner ; I call out, " Who is there ?"

No one answers.   No doubt he is crouching for a spring.

I am slightly agitated, and the revolver somehow goes off.

The ladies shriek. Then there is a momentary silence.

"Have you killed him?" asks ROSE ANNA. Perhaps I have.

We look into the room. No one is there. The fact is, we had forgotten to put out the moderateur, which we burn now instead of the gas.

CHAPTER XV

POPKINS for the last ever so long has been in the habit of drawing me aside, and saying in a confidential manner, "You'll come and dine with me, old boy, one day, won't you?"

I assure him with true and heartfelt fervour that I will. Then I pause, expecting a special invitation, but none coming, I ask, "When?"

He answers, "Oh, in a day or two—say next week."

We say next week, and then the matter drops.

It is worthy of remark that this has been going on for nearly two months.

At last he gives me a special invitation. I accept, at which he seems a little surprised, and mutters something about his having been afraid I

The above represents MR. FULLALOVE and his sporting friend in the act of giving 3 to 2 bar 1 ; or perhaps, MR. FULLALOVE thinks, it may have been 4 to 1 bar 2. At any rate it was bar something. MR. FULLALOVE feels quite certain about the bar.

might have a previous engagement. I say emphatically I have nothing of the kind, but he does not seem reassured.

I leave word with ROSE ANNA not to sit up, as we may probably have one of my roaring evenings, and I ride into town thinking of the dinner, and imagining a sumptuous bill of fare.

POPKINS and I leave COUTER AND PHLIMSY'S arm-in-arm. We walk on for about three-quarters of an hour, and then POPKINS asks where we had better dine. I thought he was taking me to his lodgings, and the shock of this question, coming upon an empty stomach, and a pair of tight-boots, makes me reel.

He suggests some half-dozen of the most noted and most expensive of the London hotels. I say, eagerly, whichever he likes. He doesn't seem to like any. He gives a capital reason why we should not go to one, and a really excellent excuse for stopping away from the rest.

I am in a measure convinced; but my appetite is whetted rather than appeased by the way in which he talks of clear turtle, fricandeau au something, and cotelettes à la something else; bottles of sparkling hock, fowls, salads, Stilton, and a glass or two of port to follow.

We retrace our steps till we are getting near COUTER AND PHLIMSY'S again, when POPKINS

grasps my arm tightly, and says he'll tell me what
—he's tired of French kickshaws and thingummies;
let's have a change, and dine off a quiet chop and
mashed potatoes.

I make bold to tell him I prefer French cookery.
He hesitates for a moment, and then cries, " Come
along, then ; we'll dine at the Café de la Lune."

Again we turn round, and trudge another weary
twenty minutes, and, after much agony and the
threading of many slums, we reach the café, situ-
ated in a narrow, noisy, dirty street, enter by a
swing door, and take our seats in a sort of
tunnel.

Hereupon I say, with a long breath, " Now to
begin."

But this is not to be yet awhile.   POPKINS says,
"I'm hardly hungry enough, and the dinner's on
the *table d'hôte* style."

For my part, I am half famished.

I ask, " What do you propose ?"

"The proper thing," he says, " is sherry and
bitters—or, stop, we'll do it in the French style.
You like absinthe, of course ?"

I reply, " Of course—of course," and wonder
what the dickens he is going to give me.   POPKINS
then summons a waiter, and addresses him in
French.

The waiter seems surprised.   He puts his head

on one side, with a bird-like movement, and inquires, in English, what POPKINS is pleased to
want? When POPKINS tells him, he seems more
surprised than ever, and, as well as I can understand, wants us to go somewhere else and get it.
I begin to think POPKINS has been trying to show
off, and is making a fool of himself.

I am still more of this opinion when his order
is presently executed. The waiter brings two tum-
blers, in each of which stands a small liqueur-glass-
ful of green-looking fluid. He puts a water bottle
down beside it, and retires.

I watch POPKINS narrowly, and observe that he
does not know what to do next. For my part
I am in the profoundest ignorance upon the
subject.

After a moment's pause, he says, " How do you
usually take it?"

I reply, in my most artful manner, "There's
only one way, is there?"

He says, "Oh! how do you mean?"

This is growing ridiculous.

After some hesitation POPKINS says, "I shall
take a little water with it."

He does, and makes a face. I try mine neat,
and make a worse face. I also cough.

POPKINS says, "Not bad?"

"Oh, no," I answer; "first rate."

Eventually we gulp down the horrible mess, somehow or other, and then, at last, POPKINS orders the dinner.

To the accompaniment of an incessant clicking of billiard balls, and with the seasoning of a faint odour of tobacco, I suppose we are about to commence our repast.

It is not what might be called sumptuous, neither is it exactly what I had expected from a person of POPKINS'S taste; nevertheless it is very good, and I am too hungry to be particular. The thin claret placed by our side does not suit our palate. POPKINS suggests beer, and then, as if seized with a sudden notion, says, "I tell you what, old fellow. You stand a bottle of wine!"

I don't catch at this idea quite as readily as I might, but as he is standing the dinner, I can't exactly refuse.

I tell him to order what he likes. He takes me at my word, and calls for a bottle of champagne.

Our spirits revive somewhat after this. I make a joke, at which POPKINS laughs heartily.

POPKINS is one of those few fellows who can appreciate a bit of quiet humour. We conclude a good meal with a cup of coffee, and then call for the bill.

" Ah !" says POPKINS, "very reasonable.

" Champagne, ten shillings—that's your affair,

my boy; two dinners, four shillings—hum! two shillings apiece ; coffee sixp——bother! I'll stand coffee.

"Let's see, FULLALOVE. You pay twelve-and-
six, and I'll—No, hang it, it isn't worth breaking into
a five-pound note ; you pay the lot and I'll owe it
you, and—yes, of course—I must have a cab.
Lend us half-a-crown till to-morrow."

I don't quite fancy MR. POPKINS will induce me
to spend any more evenings with him just yet
awhile. After all, ROSE ANNA is sitting up.

*   *   *   *   *

When I reach home an hour or two later, we
have words.

*   *   *   *   *

Says POPKINS to me, a few days afterwards,
"Join our sweep."

I tell him I am not in the habit of joining myself to anybody, and that to go about in a Siamese
twin fashion with a sweep is about the last thing I
should think of.

He laughs and says what a wag I am. I laugh
too. I have noticed that I am generally most
waggish unintentionally. POPKINS goes on to explain he means a Derby sweep. I say, "Oh! ah!
to be sure," wondering the while what difference
there is between a Derby and a London sweep;

but my eyes are soon opened, and I part with the half-sovereign, which was to have gone towards ROSE ANNA'S new bonnet, for a share in the sweep which my friend POPKINS is getting up.

They throw a lot of little papers into two hats, and then pick them out again one by one.

" MR. FULLALOVE," cries one.

" Lady Elizabeth," says another.

I answer to my name, but Lady Elizabeth does not ; indeed there are no ladies in the room.

POPKINS gives me two little scraps of paper pinned together, and slaps me on the back, and says I'm in luck. Presently he asks whether I mean to "stand" or "hedge." I hesitate, but at last summon up courage to tell him I don't know anything about sporting matters, and ask his advice.

He says he'll tell me what to do, and, in a mysterious whisper, adds, " Make a book."

Seeing me hesitate, he repeats, in a still more mysterious whisper, " Take the odds."

I say, "All right," and ask where they are to be got. He says, leave that to him, and I leave it accordingly.

The day before the Derby I see him again. He is in high spirits, and shows me a multitude of hieroglyphics in a little memorandum book, and says, " See what I've done for you. You can't

lose, and you may win a couple of hundred or
so."

Book-making appears to be a lucrative pro-
fession. Why didn't I begin it earlier in life? I
might by this time have made a fortune.

POPKINS tells me I must go to Epsom and see
the race, so I ask leave of COUTER, who scowls and
refers me to PHLIMSY. PHLIMSY says he hopes
I don't bet, and gives me permission to absent myself, though not willingly.

We go down by train, and are squashed and
pushed and shoved about in a most disgusting
manner.

We reach Epsom very hot, and have a dusty
walk up to the course. We are implored to buy
sporting papers, pipe lights, "c'rect cards," and
choice cigars; we are besought to give half-pence
to scores of jolly-looking mendicants; and we are
addressed indifferently as "my lords," "gallant
captains," and "noble sportsmen."

This, however flattering it may be, palls upon
one by repetition. We go into BARNARD'S stand.
POPKINS kindly explains everything to me. He
shows me the BISHOP OF LONDON rushing about
frantically, yelling, " I'll bet odds! I'll bet odds!"

MR. SPURGEON is also there, and wants, as
well as I can make out, to give 3 to 2 bar 1. Upon
reflection it may be 4 to 2 bar 2. Indeed, I'm not

very clear what it is; but he seems much excited, and wears a gilt hat.

I am excited also, though I don't exactly know why, and feel inclined to give something to something bar something else, though I have not the remotest notion what it means.

POPKINS says I had better back a certainty he knows of. Why not? I wonder, though, how I am to do it.

Hullo! Somebody says they're off. What a row they make! I can't see a bit. "Here they come!" Where? I wish I was a lanky one, and could see over little chaps. "Hats off!" I'm not quite quick enough, for some one tips mine off from behind.

I see it bobbing from one to another.

"I'll have your hat," they say, and they have it. "Here they are!" Somebody leans on my shoulders. He leans very heavily, and presses me down as though I were a jack being pressed into a box.

While I am below the surface the horses go by. After it is over I struggle up again, and begin to look for the gentleman who has got my hat. I can't find him though.

POPKINS seizes hold of me. "What are you doing?" he says. "Don't you see you've won?"

"Didn't see anything," I reply, "and I don't see my hat."

"Oh, hang your hat!" he says; "come and get your money."

It seems that a gentleman in a purple coat and a gamboge waistcoat owes me fifty pounds, but upon POPKINS mentioning the fact, he becomes abusive. As well as I can understand, he wants our ticket, and we don't seem to have one. POP-KINS says to me, "What have you done with it?" I don't recollect having had it. If I ever had it, it is gone now; so is some loose silver, and my watch.

I am horrified by this discovery, and entreat POPKINS to come away and let us go home. But he won't, and the gentleman in the gamboge waistcoat calls him, as well as I can catch the word, "a Welshman."

I am at a loss to understand his meaning, for POPKINS is a Londoner, if ever there was one; but the bystanders seem greatly excited by this infor-mation. "Turn him out!" they cry; and a mo-ment afterwards POPKINS is seized upon by an infuriated mob.

They tear and rend POPKINS, so to speak. I observe that POPKINS'S hat goes in one direction, and POPKINS himself goes in another. If I were strong enough I would rescue him; but I am not. Finally he is ejected.

I go to look for him, and find him much the

worse for his mauling. Indeed he seems to be pulled to pieces. Eventually, having no money, we walk home.

I have done with the turf for the present, if you have no objection.

MRS. MANTOWLER *wants to know who is singing, and* ROSE ANNA *wants to know what it all means.*

MR. FULLALOVE *is undecided which portion of the 16th chapter this picture shall be said to illustrate. In this style, was it the custom of the* ROSE ANNA *of his bosom to entreat him to buy her so many things?* MR. FULLALOVE *is supposed to be in the act of wavering. Subsequently it is needless to say he was lost.*

CHAPTER XVI.

WE GO IN FOR SEVERAL THINGS AND VISIT THE OPERA.

MRS. MANTOWLER and ROSE ANNA have gone out for the day. I saw them start in the early morning in a pony chaise, MRS. MANTOWLER driving. It has struck me several times, that if I could obtain a few private lessons from that lady in manly accomplishments, I might get on better than I do. It may be humiliating, but I fear it's true.

I pass my day as usual, and go home at the customary hour. I call for my dinner, and the servant says, "Missis didn't say nuffin about dinner." Neither, it appears, did Missis say when she'd be home.

With the promptitude of a master mind, I direct a meal to be obtained from the nearest cookshop, with all speed.

Our servant, with a grin, asks, "where I'll be pleased to have it?"

With majesty I answer, "In the dining-room, of course."

She replies, "that, if I please, MR. COMPO and his men are at work there, and the place is all of a huproar."

With less majesty I suggest the drawing-room.

She's been a-cleaning of it out, she says, and it's all of a rumpus.

Finally, after much talk, in which she shows less respect for my position as master of the house than I could wish, she reveals to me that the only place where I can hope to eat my meal in peace is on the staircase. She also mentions, incidentally, that, she has just washed the stairs down, but that she should imagine some of them must be nearly dry.

In the end, I do manage to get my dinner—after a fashion; and then, being fairly driven from the premises by the smell of soap and water, I go out into the garden and inspect the progress MR. COMPO and his men are making.

It seems to me a favourable opportunity for asserting myself master of the house, and proprietor of the embryo conservatory. I take my stand upon a plank on the top of a heap of wet sticky clay, which has been dug from the foundation of the billiard-room, and, in a commanding voice, ask how they are getting on down there.

MR. COMPO thanks me, and says, "Nicely."

While I am thinking what to say next, a voice behind, of a gruff and unmusical character, says,—

"By your leave, guv'nor."

I look round and see a burly herculean navvy charging at me with a barrowload of bricks. He comes straight towards me, never slackening his pace. If I remain in my present position I shall be shot over into the pit with the bricks; if I turn I only rush upon my fate; if I leave the plank it can only be to tread the soft clayey mud by which I am surrounded.

I choose the latter alternative. I step on to the clay. I go down, down, down, till I think I shall disappear altogether. I call for help. I hear suppressed laughter.

COMPO says I've put my foot in it.

He comes to help me, and sticks in the clay alongside.

He suggests we look like a couple of cabbages all a-blowing and a-growing.

Somehow or other we both get out after a time. I come out without my left-hand boot. COMPO, who's in a suit of corduroy, treats it as a good joke.

I, who have just paid four pounds fifteen for an Oxford mixture suit, don't see the point of it.

I sit down—on a trowel, first, subsequently on a pile of bricks—and with a penknife try to scrape off the yellow clay. COMPO, meanwhile, fishes for and catches my boot.

"All right, sir," says COMPO; "it'll brush off when it's dry."

I don't believe it ever will be dry, and I tell him so.

He says he doesn't know about that, but he's sure that *he* is precious dry.

After a pause, he wishes, in a mournful tone, that he had the price of a pint of beer about him.

I take no notice of this, nor of three subsequent hints from each of the three men.

I begin, after that, to find myself in the way. Wherever I go, some one wants to wheel a barrow. Bricks fall on my corns, mortar splashes my coat, and I think I'd better go in.

As I pass beneath the scaffold, some one says, "Below!" I say "Hullo!" and look up.

A huge dab of plaster descends upon my head, and I hear a tittering and guffawing all round.

If I thought it had been done on purpose, I'd ——. I'm terrible when I'm roused, as I've mentioned before; and I'm very nearly roused now.

I glare round, but I notice the "navvies" are all about six feet one; so I don't rouse myself further, but subside, go upstairs, and change my damaged clothing.

I must do something to pass the evening, so I try cleaning my garments to kill the time. I try water and a towel first. The towel I make in a terrible mess; the garments, from being spotty, become smeary. A streak of yellow clay, a streak of whitewash, a patch of the original material, and a lump of mud is the motley garb I wear.

The more I scrub the worse things get. I try a nailbrush and yellow soap, and get in a lather. No good. I try hot water and pumicestone. Worse. I rub a hole through the cloth, but still the clay won't come away.

Three towels have I reduced to a condition perfectly awful to contemplate. I upset water on the carpet, and seize a clayey towel to wipe it up. Horror! A yellow streak comes upon our new Kidderminster.

What will ROSE ANNA say?

I remember that in the closet there is a bottle of WELCHER'S Odontoscopic Fluid, for removing stains from everything. I fly to it. I empty it on the carpet. Worse horror still! The colours

o

of the carpet disappear instantly, leaving a large bald patch in the middle, just where there used to be a bunch of rhododendrons and sunflowers, particularly admired by ROSE ANNA.

I throw myself on my knees and scrub, and soap, and lather, in the hope of bringing the colour back.

While I am still engaged in this hopeless task, I hear a double knock.

ROSE ANNA and MRS. MANTOWLER have returned.

What shall I do?

*　　　*　　　*　　　*　　　*

That MRS. MANTOWLER has made a fresh discovery. I wish the woman was at the bottom of the sea, or that the male MANTOWLER, if he exists, would come and claim her.

She has found out that, besides the conservatory and billiard-room, which are approaching completion, we have another want in our little dovecot. We have no piano! ROSE ANNA has just discovered she dotes upon music; MRS. MANTOWLER declares it is the height of cruelty and barbarism to refuse her the means of gratifying her taste, especially as it would be such an amusement to her, and help to while away the hours during which I am slaving and toiling at COUTER AND PHLIMSY'S.

Does the woman think my purse is as long as her tongue? I hear of nothing but music now; but I make a firm stand, and refuse to purchase a piano. Pressed for reasons, and fairly driven to bay, I acknowledge that I have not the money to do so.

MRS. MANTOWLER laughs, and says, "Hire one on the three years' principle." I decline, but offer to give an organ-man sixpence a week to play for an hour under our windows, on certain evenings.

My proposal is treated with scorn. My firmness, I congratulate myself, has had the desired effect. The piano discussion drops, but only for a time. Next day it is renewed, enforced by a number of advertisements cut from a newspaper. "See here," says ROSE ANNA, putting half a dozen little slips of print before me. "Look at these," cries MRS. MANTOWLER, triumphantly.

I look, and find all the advertisements are to the same effect. A gentleman going abroad wants to dispose of a cottage piano, as good or better than new, at one quarter of cost price. A lady going to Scotland desires to do ditto at ditto; so does a clergyman's family in reduced circumstances; so does a lady of title, for certain domestic reasons. Upon my word, one would think pianos are going begging.

I pause, I read, I waver, I doubt, I calculate, and at last I consent to go to a certain address and inspect a piano which is to be parted with at a great sacrifice. It is the one said to be the property of a lady of title, and the address given is a back street in a far from aristocratic quarter. I knock at the lady of title's door in the course of the afternoon (it is a dirty door, by the way). A notice in the window proclaims that the house to which it belongs is to be let.

I experience some difficulty in obtaining admission. I am eyed from the window, and, I have reason to believe, through the keyhole. I am received with evident distrust, until I explain my errand, when the door flies open and I am admitted with alacrity. I am shown into a dingy room upstairs by a dingy servant. There is no carpet on the floor, and very little furniture to be seen ; but there, standing in a recess, is the object of my visit—a very elegant, handsomely carved cottage piano, ivory keys, &c., &c., as per advertisement.

A strong smell of tobacco pervades the apartment. I wonder whether the lady of title smokes. The door opens, and a man enters. He is of a Hebraic cast of countenance. He is also dingy, not to say dirty, in appearance, and diffuses alternate whiffs of onions and tobacco. Can he be the husband of the lady of title? I decide not. He is civil. He eyes me eagerly. He explains certain circumstances to account for the sale of the piano. He sits down at it and plays well and brilliantly. It seems to be really a good instrument. I am delighted, and look upon it as my own, and almost determine to learn to play myself.

We haggle about the sum a good deal, the dingy gentleman assuring me the price in the advertisement was a mistake. Ultimately he gives way. He tells me I have a spendid bargain, and agrees to send the piano to HIGHLOW Terrace, at once, and I agree to pay him the stipulated sum. So far all is well. I don't see how I can be cheated this time.

When I get home all HIGHLOW Terrace, so to speak, is gushing with melody. An empty cart is at my door, and a crowd of children are hanging on to my front railings, listening to the overture to *Masaniello*, which MRS. MANTOWLER is performing with much energy. The man who brought the piano is waiting in the passage for the money.

It strikes me that he is the same man who sold me the instrument, or else his twin brother; but as he does not recognize me, I pay him the money, and let him go. MRS. MANTOWLER is in ecstasies; ROSE ANNA is frantic with admiration. It really is a magnificent instrument, and would not have been dear at three times the price I paid for it. We are so delighted with our purchase that we go on playing till our neighbours knock at the wall, as a reminder that it is past midnight. We go to bed. I dream I compose an opera.

* * * * * *

We have had our instrument three days. I am learning my scales. We have had it tuned. The tuner declares it to be a beautiful piano. We certainly *have* got a bargain! ROSE ANNA and MRS. MANTOWLER are playing a duet; I am listening from the sofa; the greater part of HIGH-LOW Terrace is listening from the road.

A cart—one of those carts made expressly for the conveyance of pianos—stops at our door. The driver and another man knock, and are admitted.

"That's it!" says one, throwing open the drawing-room door. "There it is!" says the other, pointing to the piano.

What *can* this mean? With dignity I demand an explanation.

"That's our instrument," says the man, "and we've come for it."

I deny their right. They get boisterous, and seize hold of its legs. I produce **my** receipt.

"Well," says one, "you must be a fool to think to buy a piano like this for that money!"

Matters become serious. I learn that the man who sold it me had no right to sell; that he had hired it on the three years' system, and had only paid for one quarter. Finally, I am compelled to let the piano go. It takes its departure amidst the tears of my wife, the indignation of MRS. MAN-TOWLER, and the jeers of the crowd. One of our next door neighbours waves his hat and hurrahs frantically.

I take a cab, and a policeman, and go off at once to the place where I bought the instrument. The house is deserted. The policeman says he thinks *I* was sold, instead of the piano.

*   *   *   *   *

Assuredly it was not my fault about the piano, and I must say, after spending my money and doing my best, it is rather hard to be taunted and badgered and baited as I have been by ROSE ANNA.

MRS. MANTOWLER certainly takes my part; but there's a way with her which I don't exactly like. The fact is, it has occurred to me, more than once, she is inclined to be witty at my expense. I like a joke, but I can enjoy it better when I don't suffer in consequence. I enjoy a laugh, but I would rather not be laughed at.

Having made this short explanatory statement,
I may, perhaps, be permitted to continue the narra-
tion of the events which spring from the sudden
departure of our piano.

Day after day I am doomed to hear lamenta-
tions on the absence of that detestable instrument.
I am told that the man who has not music in his
soul is something which I cannot consider complimentary. I am also informed that music has charms
to soothe something which is still less complimentary. MRS. MANTOWLER, in a tone of withering
contempt says—

" Why you can't even whistle."

ROSE ANNA doesn't believe, she says, that I
could play the triangle. I tell her I know more
about music than she does. She says I don't, and
pouts.

MRS. MANTOWLER hits upon a bright idea.
She says, " Take us to the Opera, and let's see who
enjoys it most."

As I suppose this means that I am to pay, I
don't enter into the plan with the ardour the ladies
do ; but, as usual, after much talking and a few
tears, I have to give in, and I agree to take them
to Covent Garden.

I begin by fixing on a far-off date. As it grows
nearer, I propose an alteration. Several accidents
occur, and cause further postponements. At last,

the ladies grow impatient, and they ask, Am I ever going to take them ?

MANTOWLER wants to know whether "I mean business."

There is a slanginess about MANTOWLER that I do not admire. I sincerely trust that she will not corrupt ROSE ANNA.

Eventually the day *is* fixed, and there is no help for it. I must take the tickets. How much will they cost ? The ladies have not told me what part of the house they want to go to, but I am given to understand (for I have never been myself) that every part is very expensive, and I determine on the cheapest.

I find a bill in a bye-street, in front of an oil and colourman's, and, being short-sighted, fall into a frog-like attitude before it.

Whilst in this position, an uneducated street-boy takes advantage of my having my back turned towards him, and catches me a slap.

This causes me to grovel, and the proprietor of the shop finding me on my hands and knees embracing the play-bill board, wants to know what I am "up to ?"

However, I have obtained full particulars. I find that there are stalls at five shillings.

I consult POPKINS upon the subject, and he tells me these are amphitheatre stalls.

I ask, " Are they good ones ?"

He replies. " First rate ; but why don't you have gallery seats at half-a-crown, they are just as good ?"

I say, " Is the gallery respectable ?"

He says, " What a duffer you are !"

I conclude by this that it is respectable, and determine that we will go there.

When I get home, I find ROSE ANNA and her friend in full dress—that is to say, if it can be called full dress when you look as if you had nothing on.

The servant fetches a cab, and the Terrace takes great interest in our departure.

I say, in a loud voice, " Covent Garden !"

The cabman says, " Where, sir ?"

I repeat, " Covent Garden !"

He says, " Covent Garden Market ?"

I reply, with dignity, " The Opera !" and he drives off, evidently in doubt.

The man is, in fact, nothing better than a fool. He pulls up at the Opera, at an imposing entrance, and we enter. I discharge him, and am liberal to the party who opens the cab door. We have gone in with much rustle, and created no small sensation.

It turns out that we have made a mistake, for the gallery door is round the corner.

We go round the corner, and ROSE ANNA and I have stormy passages by the way. But I find the right door at last, and we mount the stairs.

I think at first we shall never get to the top.

MRS. MANTOWLER is several times compelled to stop for breath, and both ladies inquire indignantly at every landing where I am taking them to.

I reply, "All right;" but when we reach our destination it does not appear quite as right as I could have wished.

MRS. MANTOWLER says, "How could you have brought us here in this dress?"

ROSE ANNA adds,—

"You must be a fool!"

After all, it was POPKINS'S fault.

It seems that for another half-crown each we can go somewhere else. We accordingly go somewhere else where the audience is more select, or, at any rate, where the female portion don't wear bonnets ; and we begin to enjoy ourselves.

I never do things by halves ; and so when the day was finally fixed upon, I found out what opera it would be, and bought a book. By so doing I have been able to learn all about the plot, and I am thereby qualified to answer any questions that may arise.

Presently a question does arise, which I can't answer anyhow. While I am thinking the matter over, another arises. MRS. MANTOWLER wants to know who it is that is singing, and ROSE ANNA wishes me to explain what it all means. Upon reflection, I find I can do neither with any certainty, and say, "Hush, half a minute," in a whisper.

But when the half-minute has expired they break out again in a louder voice. I therefore give the best explanation I can, and it happens to be a wrong one.

A gentleman sitting next to us, however, very kindly sets us to rights. It appears that the opera has been changed, owing to somebody's illness, and that instead of seeing *Rigoletto* we are seeing *Don Giovanni.*

MRS. MANTOWLER withers me with a look, and then tells the gentleman she is glad we have come on a MOZART night, and that she adores MOZART'S works.

ROSE ANNA joins in the conversation, but when I try to get in a word edgeways some one behind calls out, "Hush! If you want to chatter, go outside!"

Meanwhile the opera progresses, and ROSE ANNA begins to feel thirsty and faint. I say, "What's to be done?" She replies, "Lavender lozenges;" and I go out in search of some. I make a lengthy search, and returning in the middle of the duet, try to make my way to my seat.

The audience are enraged at this conduct. Some call to me to "stand still;" others say, "Sit down!" Some are in favour of my going back again. One bald-headed gentleman, in a terrible whisper, asks how I dare?

I reply, in expressive pantomime, and with a piteous expression of face, that I only want to get back to my seat, and I can't stop where I am, and I am very sorry my boots creak so much.

At last I do get back, and the lozenges turn out to be peppermint.

After this ROSE ANNA comes on fainter than before, and we think it best to go home. We go home, therefore, and have a tremendous row in the cab.

CHAPTER XVII.

WE HAVE SOME UNPLEASANTNESS WITH MR. COMPO.

THAT conservatory and billiard-room of ours progress but slowly.

In fact, I doubt whether they progress at all, when the fact that no workmen have been near the place for a week, is taken into consideration.

There is an ugly wooden framework half-erected, which is all there is of the conservatory, and the billiard-room is as yet represented by a big hole, which I am told is the foundation.

I meet MR. COMPO one morning, just as I am hurrying off to catch the early omnibus. He touches his hat and stops me.

He says, Could I let him have a little something on account? and then he touches his hat again.

This illustration is wholly and solely allegorical. It represents the back of MRS. MANTOWLER,—*(the cause of all our misery—that is to say,* MRS. MANTOWLER *generally, not her back)—which we longed to look upon, only she wouldn't go.*

I tell him I can't do anything of the sort, but I should like to talk to him in the evening.

He doesn't touch his hat any more, but says he'll "look in," adding, in a sort of grumble, words to the effect that I'd better "look out."

Hang his impudence!

And he makes me miss the omnibus into the bargain.

In the evening he does look in. I have been preparing myself all day for this interview. Somehow or other, when the time comes, I feel a little nervous.

The fact is, I have decided upon a course of action which I know perfectly well will please nobody but myself. But am I not a lord of the creation? Am I not master of my own house? I am. Am I bound to go through the Bankruptcy Court for the sake of ROSE ANNA'S whims? I am not.

I tell MR. COMPO, with manly dignity, that I have been thinking matters over, and have come to the conclusion that I won't have a billiard-room at all, and that the sooner he fills up the hole he has dug for the foundation the better.

He stares at me, and asks if I mean it. I answer, "Of course I do." He goes on to say something about people calling themselves gentlemen, and giving themselves airs, and robbing other people of their dues.

I don't exactly follow his argument, but I perceive that he is enraged. He wants to know if I'm a-going back from my word—if I'm a-going to pay him what I owe him—if I'm a-going to recompense him for all he's done for me?

I say, "We'll have no conservatory. Fill up the hole, and send in the bill."

He declares the hole was dug by my orders, and that he'll be somethinged if he fills it up. He also adds something about wishing to put me in a hole. If he means this metaphorically, it is coarse; if literally, it is murderous. I must get rid of him without delay, as every moment he is becoming more violent.

His violence culminates in a slam of the door as he leaves the house. It makes the whole building rock; it shakes two plates from the dresser, which fall down smash and spoil the set; it wakes Rose Anna from a nap; and it frightens Mrs. Mantowler, who screams.

I am thankful, however, even at the cost of this disturbance, to get rid of Compo. He shouts an insulting farewell to me through the keyhole. He promises I shall hear from his lawyer.

I bother his lawyer, whereat he laughs fiendishly; and then I hear his steps growing fainter

and fainter in the distance. With a flushed face I
return to the drawing-room.

The ladies want to know what's the matter. I
say, "Nothing," and devoutly wish I spoke the
truth. I can't get to sleep for thinking of COMPO's
threat about his lawyer.

I wonder whether he meant it, and supposing
he did, what I'd better do ; and supposing he
didn't, what I'd better do then. I hate per-
plexities.

    *   *   *   *   *

I come home in very high spirits the day after
this interview with COMPO. It was somebody's
birthday at COUTER AND PHLIMSY'S, and somebody stood sherry.

I am happy. I kiss ROSE ANNA with vehemence ; and when she tells me there is a large
letter waiting for me, I say, "Bother letters ! let
us enjoy ourselves."

However, when I see the epistle in question, I
confess I quake.

It is big, it has an official appearance, and is
directed in a lawyer's handwriting. COMPO's
threat recurs to my mind, and my cheeriness instantly deserts me.

Tremblingly I read the document. I can't understand it properly, but, from what I can gather

from its purport, it informs me that, unless I pay into the writers' hands a sum, which is really too awful to mention, on behalf of their client, COMPO, terrible things will happen to me.

Visions of a life-long incarceration rise up before me. I suppose I turn ghastly pale, for ROSE ANNA on one side and MRS. MANTOWLER on the other clutch hold of me, and implore me to tell them what is the matter.

Somehow or other they let me slip through their fingers, and I fall in a heap on the floor, sobbing and gasping, " Ruined ! ruined !"

ROSE ANNA beseeches, implores, and entreats me to tell her all. She urges me to lay my poor head upon her shoulder and disclose the hidden cause of all my woe.

MRS. MANTOWLER says she thinks it's only my fun. (You see by this the disadvantage of being a wag. Nobody believes you're serious when you are.)

She further adds, she never knew I was so good an actor.

At this the fury of the British Lion (myself) is roused. I address her, with stately courtesy, as " Madam," and inform her that it is no joking matter.

ROSE ANNA, who has been wavering between tears and laughter, decides in favour of the former, and through her sobs hurls stinging sarcasms and biting reproaches at MRS. MANTOWLER.

That lady listens with amazement, and ultimately melts and subsides into her pocket-handkerchief.

For some moments we all three sob together, till it suddenly strikes ROSE ANNA she is ignorant of the cause of so much misery.

Her curiosity struggles with her tears, and gets the better of them, and once more she beseeches me to tell her the fatal truth.

I tell it by little bits. I emphasize it by COMPO'S lawyer's letter.

I draw a picture (mental) of myself, dragged by the stern minions of justice from the arms of my wife, and the bosom of my family. I am again affected to tears, as I describe the probable effect of a life-long incarceration in the Tower. I'm not sure that it *is* the Tower where they lock up insolvent debtors, but it sounds well to say so.

ROSE ANNA, deeply affected, throws her arms round my neck, and we mingle our tears. We continue mingling them till we hear a sort of choking noise behind us.

We turn, and catch MRS. MANTOWLER quite flushed with endeavouring to suppress her laughter. We glare at her. She is evidently

ashamed of herself. She tries to turn the laugh
into a cough. She tries to conceal it by hiding
her face in her pocket-handkerchief, but all in
vain.

ROSE ANNA waits for a few moments, and then
gives vent to a burst of eloquence of which I should
never have deemed her capable. She reproaches
her bosom friend. She says it was she (MRS.
MANTOWLER) who first incited us to conservatories and billiard-rooms. It was she who tempted
us to launch out. It was she who selfishly determined to loll in the lap of luxury at our expense.
It was she who brought ruin, disgrace, and life-long
incarceration into the happy home in HIGHLOW
Terrace.

MRS. MANTOWLER, with cutting sarcasm and
trembling voice, says,—

" Go on, dear !"

ROSE ANNA does go on. She says, "And now,
having got all you can out of us, ruined us,
blighted our young affections, scattered our bud-
ding hopes, and destroyed our peace of mind, you
turn round and laugh at us. MRS. MANTOWLER,
we've nourished a viper, and it's stung the hand
that fed it !"

MRS. MANTOWLER doesn't seem impressed, but
she is evidently angry. She says, " Nonsense !"
and stamps her foot.

Rose Anna turns to me, and asks me, indignantly, if I'm going to allow such language to be used to my wife?

It appears to me the language has been rather the other way; however, I reply, "Certainly not, my dear."

"Then," continues Rose Anna, "bid that—that—scorpion—take her departure!"

Mrs. Mantowler, with the sweetest smile on her face, comes and places her hand on my shoulder:—

"Never mind what she says, *dear* Mr. Fullalove," she tells me; "wait till she is calm."

Rose Anna's indignation knows no bounds; she says she's ashamed of Mrs. Mantowler, that she wishes she had never set eyes on her, and hopes she never may after to-day; she adds that she never thought her a woman of much principle, but that she should dare, after all that had passed, to make love to *me*, surpassed belief!

I don't see this myself.

Mrs. Mantowler, however, indignantly repudiates the notion of making love to me. She says she always hated monkeys. I don't see what monkeys have to do with it, but the allusion makes Rose Anna still more indignant.

The ladies get so very warm in their quarrel, that I think seriously of calling in the police.

First one and then the other appeals to me to take her part. I am confused, bewildered, and amazed. I don't know anything about anything, but—as the safest plan—agree with both indiscriminately.

This answers for a little while, but at last both turn upon me, and I am assailed with such a flood of eloquence, none of it, on either side, being of a complimentary nature, that I seek to make my escape. I am pursued. I am told I ought to be ashamed of myself so repeatedly, that at last I begin to feel that I have done something wrong.

I fly from the house in desperation, and take a walk round the brickfield. When at last I venture back to HIGHLOW Terrace, I feel some misgivings that there may have been bloodshed during my absence. I enter by the back door softly. All is still. I creep with a palpitating heart to the drawing-room.

There, to my surprise, I see ROSE ANNA and MRS. MANTOWLER with their arms round each other's waists, kissing and whispering as of old, only more so.

They look up and scowl at me when I enter. I address them cheerily, they answer gloomily. I make inquiries, and only get monosyllabic replies.

What does this mean ? Will anybody tell me what I have done ?

I am glad the two ladies should be friends again ; still I do not exactly see why I should be made a victim. I pass a most miserable evening, and when, at last, I get to bed and sleep I dream of COMPO and the lawyers' letter.

CHAPTER XVIII.

I HAVE MY REVENGE UPON THE MAN NEXT DOOR.

ROSE ANNA says I have no spirit. I'll tell you how it comes about.

At the back of our house is a narrow strip of garden. At the back of my next-door neighbour's house there is a similar narrow strip running side by side with ours. He grows cabbages, or mangel-wurzel, or something, in his strip. We grow sickly roses and weedy geraniums in ours.

He has an antipathy to slugs and snails, and every morning of his life he makes the tour of his cabbages, searching for devouring reptiles. So far I have no fault to find. He discovers the creatures by the bushel. The early gardener gets the slug. He picks them off, and gets rid of them from his own premises by pitching them over the low wall into mine.

ROSE ANNA *may be here observed asking* MR. FULLALOVE *if he is going to allow himself to be trodden on by the next door neighbour. The next door neighbour is six foot two inches high, and double* MR. FULLALOVE'S *weight—but these are trifling details.*

He asks me how I dare throw snails into his garden. I tell him the snails in Highlow Terrace are the most wonderful jumpers I ever saw.

This is what I object to. Our neighbour's cabbages are first-rate, but our roses suffer.

ROSE ANNA is indignant, and wants me to be indignant too. Women are so unreasonable. I feel that if my neighbour were a foot or two shorter, and possessed of a mild, good-natured countenance, I should be very indignant; but as he is six-feet-two in his stockings, broad in proportion, and with cross and pugnacious features, I consider it better to take no notice of his proceedings.

ROSE ANNA won't see it in this light. She appeals to her bosom friend, and MRS. MANTOWLER says I ought to take steps. Early in the morning I leave my downy couch for the purpose of taking steps, and repair stealthily to the garden. There is my neighbour scrunching about among his cabbages; presently a slug drops at my feet. A minute later a shower of snails descends upon my gravel walk.

It certainly *is* time I took steps. Now is the moment for decisive action. I collect the snails and slugs, and when, by the sound of his creaking boots, I conclude my neighbour to be far away, I commence pitching the slimy creatures back again into his domain.

Some one says, " Hullo, there!" and I hide under the wall. The next minute the snails return to my garden.

This is not to be borne. We are regularly playing battledore ´and shuttlecock with snails. I pitch them back. I feel pleased when I hear one—a whopper he is—descend on the glass of a forcing frame, and by the sound crack a pane.

I feel still more pleased when I hear a violent exclamation as I throw another. I chuckle to myself, for I feel sure I have hit the bloated cabbage-grower with one of his own reptiles.

I leave off chuckling, and don't feel nearly so pleased when I hear a sound as if my next-door neighbour were struggling to climb the little wall which separates our gardens.

Remembering his huge stature and enormous bulk, I may say I tremble, and for a moment meditate flight ; but as you are aware, I am never at a loss, so, abandoning the notion of retreat, I assume innocency.

Seizing a spade, I suddenly commence working hard at the centre bed — the pride of ROSE ANNA'S heart. I assume a careless, negligent air. I hum a tune, and endeavour to appear at my ease. ¦

A gruff voice from the top of the wall addresses me, as "You, sir !" and adds, " Hullo !"

Looking up, I perceive an infuriated face intently regarding me. He wants to know if I hear.

I fancy I had better reply, so I inform him that it's a fine morning, and hope he and his cabbages are both well. I mean this to be conciliatory, but he considers it insulting.

He uses bad language. He asks me how I dare throw slugs and snails over into his garden; he informs me a snail hit him on the forehead. I tell him the snails in HIGHLOW Terrace are some of the most wonderful jumpers I ever saw. He evidently does not believe me.

He disappears for a few minutes, and then showers the horrid things back upon me. Savagely he declares, that if as much as one snail jumps over his wall from my garden, he'll give me the soundest thrashing I ever had in my life!

This is getting serious. If I permit this conduct to pass unnoticed, he will set me down for a coward.

I think for some moments, searching in the corners of my brain for a crushing repartee. Just as I have thought of one he goes indoors and shuts the door with a bang.

Revenge! Ha! ha! But I must dissemble.

I dissemble so well that neither my next-door neighbour, my wife, nor my wife's friend, know anything about it.

I go at the proper hour to COUTER AND

PHLIMSY'S—still dissembling—(on the knifeboard of the omnibus); but when I find myself alone with POPKINS, I let my passion find a vent.

I repeat "Blood!" several times in a ferocious tone.

POPKINS says, "Don't—try poison!"

He adds, he knows a deadly drug, which, if I have a spite against anybody, will make them feel particularly uncomfortable without killing them.

Will it lose its properties by boiling? I ask, a sudden idea striking me, and a fiendish glare of satisfaction lighting up my face.

He says he doesn't see why it should.

Ha! ha! Revenge on my next-door neighbour! He's only just come, and I don't know his name. He loves cabbages. I send for the finest in Covent Garden Market. POPKINS purchases his deadly drug.

Together we doctor the vegetable, dropping the fluid in between its leaves.

Then we get a boy, pay his omnibus fare, and give him sixpence to leave the cabbage at the house next door to mine in HIGHLOW Terrace.

The whole of that day I can scarcely do any work for chuckling and giggling.

My next-door neighbour shall learn what it is to throw his slugs and snails into my garden, and then bully me!

Ha! ha! Revenge!

*   *   *   *   *

When I go home my neighbour is not in his garden. Possibly he is gorged with drugged cabbage.

I look up at his bedroom window, and observe the blind is down. I chuckle and rub my hands with delight. At dinner we have a cabbage.

I can scarcely restrain myself from yelling and shrieking with laughter at the thought of the similar vegetable next door.

I eat of it and enjoy it, although I nearly choke myself over every mouthful, as the thought of my revenge comes sweet upon me.

At last ROSE ANNA'S patience is exhausted, and she insists upon knowing why I am going on in that absurd manner.

I give up dissembling, and tell her the whole truth about the medicated vegetable. MRS. MAN-TOWLER turns ghastly pale.

ROSE ANNA puts down her fork and leans back in her chair, while she gasps, "Tell me—tell me, if you love me—had the boy who took the cabbage red hair?"

"He had!"

"Did he squint?"   ()

"He did."

"Oh!" cries MRS. MANTOWLER, rushing from the table.

"Murderer!" shrieks ROSE ANNA, "you have poisoned your own wife! The miscreant you hired to accomplish your fiendish purpose brought the cabbage to the wrong house!!"

"Where—where did he bring it?"

"Here—you yourself have eaten more than half of it!!!"

Oh! I do feel so ill! I go upstairs and lie down; so does ROSE ANNA; so does MRS. MAN-TOWLER.

We all want to get to sleep, and none of us can, because that horrid neighbour of ours is out in his garden, singing, "We always are so jolly, O!" at the top of his disgusting voice.

He said with a smile that he was JONES, *and wanted me to sub-scribe to the "British Poets."*

ROSE ANNA *may be here observed studying a manual on* Cro
quet. *She was wonderfully up in the rules. Indeed if our lawn
had ever been in a proper condition to play upon, I have no doubt*
ROSE ANNA *would have been a first-rate player—but alas, it never
was in a proper condition.*

CHAPTER XIX.

I TAKE IN THE "BRITISH POETS" AND PRACTISE THE GAME OF CROQUET.

SOME time ago—months, or perhaps it is even years—a very gentlemanly man called in upon me at my lodgings, and asked if I would subscribe to an illustrated edition of the "British Poets."

I was at the time a bachelor, and lived in furnished lodgings. Somehow the gentlemanly man found out my name, and came and called on me. At the moment he arrived, I was partaking of a meat tea. The meat I had brought home from a neighbouring ham-and-beef shop, and it was still in the paper.

Being a hot day, I had, for comfort's sake, taken off my coat, waistcoat, and boots ; and, as yet, I had not put on my slippers. These combined circumstances caused me some confusion when the gen-

tlemanly man was shown in upon me suddenly
and came forward with a smiling face and a low
bow.

Under the impression that he was a friend of
mine, I shook hands with him heartily. Finding
out, when I had done, that he was not the
friend I at first had taken him for, I felt embar-
rassed.

From what he said, however, I concluded that
though he was not that friend, he was another. I
therefore shook hands again, still more heartily.
Eventually it turned out that he was not the other
friend either, and I asked him who the deuce he
was?

He said, with a smile, that he was JONES, of
JENKINS AND JONES'S, and that he wanted me to
subscribe to the " British Poets."

I replied that I did not think I should like to
do so.

He said, " Why not ?" and I found it difficult
to explain.

He told me the book was " dirt cheap," and
showed me the engravings, executed at a fabulous
cost.

I replied that I did not care for pictures, and
never, by any chance, read poetry.

This seemed to grieve as much as it astonished
him. He said he could not believe it in a gen-

tleman of my education and high social position.

Then he laughed, and nudged me in the
ribs. There was no doubt about it—I must be
joking.

I was obliged to admit that I was joking,
though I really wasn't ; and, in the end, I did sub-
scribe to the "British Poets," and signed a paper
to the effect that I would pay two shillings a
month for a monthly portion of the work, which
was to be supplied to me until the book should
reach its conclusion.

The whole transaction was extremely business-
like, except in one particular — I neglected to
ascertain how many monthly parts there were to be.

As I said at the beginning, it may be years
ago since the gentlemanly man first called upon
me. Since then he has paid me periodical visits,
and I have paid him many sums of two shillings,
and the "British Poets" keep on coming out, and
there seems no likelihood of them ever coming to
an end.

For some time I read the poets as they ap-
peared. Getting a little in arrear, however, I con-
tented myself by glancing at the general contents
of the monthly portion. For many months, now,
I have done no more than look at the pictures.

That is to say, I have also looked at the bottom of the last page, to see if there were any signs of a conclusion. As a general rule, however, the number leaves off in the middle of a sentence.

ROSE ANNA has never taken kindly to the "Poets." She not only won't read them, but she will not allow them to lie on the side-table in the drawing-room. She says they are "litter."

Owing to this objection on ROSE ANNA'S part, I keep the "British Poets" upstairs in a box under our bed, and when a new number comes out, I put it away with the rest as quickly as possible. Not quickly enough, however, to avoid ROSE ANNA'S eagle eye.

She says, "What, more rubbish?"

I say, "It isn't rubbish. You know nothing about it. No gentleman's library is complete without a copy of the 'British Poets.'"

She says, "But you haven't got a library. Where are the other books?"

To a certain extent this is correct. I have not more than a dozen other volumes, and, strictly speaking, all these are not mine, if their owners ever ask for them back again. Nevertheless, I observe—

"I will have the 'British Poets' bound, and then perhaps you will think them worthy of a place on the drawing-room table."

Rose Anna looks more favourably upon the
" Poets" after this, and says,—

" Is the book complete ?"

" Yes," I reply. " This is a double number,
containing the title-page," and I show the monthly
part, artfully concealing the price (four shillings for
a double number) with my thumb.

Rose Anna looks at the book, and utters a
cry of derision. It appears that, after all, this is
only the end of the first volume. The publication
of the " British Poets," will probably go on till the
crack of doom.

    *   *   *   *   *

Next day, at my office, the gentlemanly man
calls on me and asks if I have all the back num-
bers, and do I want them bound ?

I say I do, for they are of no use as they are.
He says he can get them bound for me very
cheaply, and names an extremely low price. I
jump at the offer, and bring up the parts next
morning in a parcel. He takes them away, and I
see no more of him.

I do not know his address. I wait patiently.
Weeks roll on. The day of calling comes round,
but he does not call.

It is my firm conviction that I have been DONE !

    *   *   *   *

We have had a good deal of consultation up in HIGHLOW Terrace.

Matters have assumed a pleasanter aspect. There has been a good deal of kissing and some tears, and now we are all right again.

COMPO'S lawyers' letter has been answered, and to such effect that our landlord agrees to do anything and everything in reason. The hole representing the billiard-room has been filled up and turfed over, and MRS. MANTOWLER, seized with one of those marvellous inspirations for which she is famous, says, with her characteristic energy, "The very thing for croquet!" and ROSE ANNA declares with vehemence that the object of her life is about to be accomplished.

MRS. MANTOWLER supposes, of course, we know how to play. We say, "Oh, yes," and then meditate for a few moments, and add, "if not, we can soon learn."

MRS. MANTOWLER offers to teach us, and ROSE ANNA wants to telegraph to Regent Street for a box of implements, to be sent immediately by special messenger.

As it is only an hour short of midnight, this cannot be done, and it is settled that I am to bring the box with me on the top of the omnibus the next afternoon.

leave COUTER AND PHLIMSY'S earlier than

usual, and purchase a beautiful set of croquet, and then mount my omnibus in triumph. At the corner of our road, ROSE ANNA is waiting in eager expectancy. Over our garden-gate leans MRS. MANTOWLER, in eagerer expectancy.

We promise a small boy twopence to carry the box up to the house. He lets it drop twice, the second time breaking the top off, and then asks for threepence.

Between us we carry all the implements on to the croquet lawn. The turf is not in that condition which I should like to see ; but, considering it's only been put down four days, it isn't *very* lumpy. The awkward part of it is, the two ladies have been watering it all the morning to make it grow, and that wherever there was an indentation there is now a puddle.

MRS. MANTOWLER undertakes to put in the hoops. We stand by in a state of eagerness watching her, and trying to look as if we knew all about it. When the arrangements are completed, acting under the directions of our instructress, we choose balls and mallets, and commence our game. MRS. MANTOWLER tells us what to do, and we do it more or less—generally less. After we've acted up to her instructions, and got in a good position for our hoop, she follows and knocks us away.

She says, "That's croquet," but she won't let us do it to her ; so it seems as if she were playing and we were not, which, considering the hammers and mallets, and sticks and turf, are all our property, seems also rather hard. The only point about it is, that MRS. MANTOWLER has a very pretty foot, and—(ROSE ANNA is looking over my shoulder, and says I am not to go on).

At last we get a chance to croquet MRS. MAN-TOWLER, and we determine with many chuckles to avail ourselves of it. ROSE ANNA tries first and hits the turf, knocking up a huge lump.

I say, "Let me try, my dear," with an air of conscious superiority.

I poise myself gracefully, and give the ladies a short lecture in the style I have heard at the Royal Polytechnic as to cause and effect, the angles of incidence, centrifugal force, &c., &c., &c. I then proceed to illustrate my remarks by an experiment. By the way, I'm not sure I am right in all my long words, but I go as near to the right ones as I can.

I raise the mallet, prepared to wreak a terrible vengeance on our instructress. I swing the mallet; it descends with all my force upon my foot instead of the ball.

MRS. MANTOWLER claps her hands, ROSE ANNA laughs, I limp. Somebody else laughs—

many somebody elses—and then I notice that we have been taking our croquet lessons in public.

I call to the ladies to come in.

They say, " Presently."

I bathe my foot in cold water, and lie on the sofa. By-and-by we have a long talk on the merits of the game. I think it very stupid, but am afraid to say so.

We go to bed early.

I have been asleep about an hour when ROSE ANNA awakens me by a violent shaking. I wake in a tremble, and ask what's the matter?

She says, " Hush !"

This is mysterious. I ask a reason for her conduct. In a thrilling whisper she says, " Don't you hear it ?"

I venture to inquire what I am expected to hear, upon which she says " Hush !" a second time in a more mysterious and thrilling manner than before.

This is really alarming. I feel I am turning pale.

" There !" says ROSE ANNA, after a pause "There it is again !—I thought it was, and now I'm sure of it."

" What, dearest — what ? Speak, I adjure you !"

My adjuration is made with chattering teeth, I confess. ROSE ANNA answers with a laugh—

"Why, you stupid old man, don't you hear it's raining?"

I feel small. I leave off teeth-chattering and take to sniggering.

I say, "Suppose it's raining, what then?"

She says, "Why, we've left all the croquet things out in the garden."

I observe, "Well?"

She continues, "You know, dear, they might spoil; I do wish you'd rouse yourself, and go and bring them in."

This is pleasant. One o'clock on a rainy morning to go down stairs, unbolt everything, and collect a miscellaneous assortment of croquet tools, and bring them in.

However, it's no use refusing, for ROSE ANNA insists. I tumble into a few things, I stumble down stairs, and out into a sloppy garden, where I trip over a hoop, and fall prostrate.

I limp back with as many of the balls and mallets as I can find, and get into bed again.

I awake in an hour's time with a violent fit of sneezing. I knew how it would be.

I've got one of my bad colds, and all owing to that confounded croquet.

Perhaps there has been no honeymoon, or it has been a honeymoon with no honey in it.

AU REVOIR, ROSE ANNA.

N.B.—The publisher of this little volume would scorn to take a mean advantage of the reader by here advertising a forthcoming work. "Mais," as our lively neighbours say, "nous verrons."

CHAPTER XX.

WE START FOR A HOLIDAY, REACH A CRISIS, TURN OVER ANOTHER NEW LEAF, AND MAKE A BAD ENDING.

ROSE ANNA and I have been getting on very well lately.

She has not cried the whole of this last week.

I am, I confess, rather at a loss to account for this phenomenon ; but an explanation presents itself after awhile. The fact is, ROSE ANNA has set her heart upon something.

Having acknowledged thus much, she asks me to guess what it is. With my customary insight into feminine nature, I reply, without a moment's hesitation—

"A bonnet."

She shakes her head, though a moment after she remarks her best *is* certainly getting shabby.

She asks me to guess again.

With much trepidation I hazard, "A silk dress."

She answers, "No, dear; though I *do* wish I had one."

With an increasing fear, I stammer, "Jewellery."

Again she shakes her head; and though my anxiety on this score is relieved, I cannot but fear it is something yet more expensive she requires.

She still wishes me to guess. I try successively silver teapots, parrots, pony-chaises, Bath buns, diamond necklaces, and a boy in buttons; but she shakes her head at all of them like a Mrs. Chinese Mandarin.

I beseech her to tell me what she requires. She laughs, and then seizes my ear in playful ferocity and kisses the tip of my nose. I intreat her, by all she holds most dear, to reveal the truth. She says she will. She remains silent for some moments, and then tells me it's very hot.

I point out to her that this is sophistry, and not argument. She says she knows that as well as I do.

Another pause. She asks me whether I don't think it must be very pleasant at the sea-side this hot weather.

This is the entrance to a trap. I do not perceive it, and say, " Delightful !"

Husbands, need I say more ? Married men, do ye not perceive what is to follow ? Bachelors, take heed ! Gay young sparks, unfettered by womankind, bewail the fate of your unhappy FULLA-LOVE.

ROSE ANNA has set her heart on a fortnight "by the sad sea waves," and I dare not say her nay.

She produces her account-books, and proves it will be a saving. She intreats ; she commands. I am obliged to give way, and ere I sleep I am forced into a promise to get two weeks' leave from COUTER AND PHLIMSY, and spend them where the " broad Atlantic laps the coral strand."

(N.B. This is ROSE ANNA'S quotation, not mine. She thinks it's BYRON ; but isn't sure.)

You, ye British public, who rejoice in living in a land of freedom, should see COUTER'S face when I ask for a fortnight's holiday. He refers me to PHLIMSY. PHLIMSY says I may stop away altogether if I like.

This is truly kind. I thank him, and say perhaps I will take three weeks. I wonder what it is he swears at when I leave the room.

I find that ROSE ANNA cannot possibly go to the sea-side without new dresses, and hats, and a hundred other articles. I never knew anything go like my money.

At last the day comes on which we have fixed to start. ROSE ANNA gets up at six to pack. She packs the greater part of her possessions into four boxes, and then finds she must have a fifth for absolute necessaries.

I point out to her that this is a good deal to take for three weeks, and ask her to bear in mind that I shall want my portmanteau. She says that's nonsense; that a brush and comb in my pocket, and a second coat over my arm, is all I need take.

It seems certainly as if we were doomed to meet with misadventure. The cab-horse which is taking us to the railway station, tumbles down, and is so long in getting up again, that we miss our train.

We have three hours to wait for the next.

ROSE ANNA suggests ices in the refreshment-room, as a pleasant way of passing the time. We find an hour and a half of ices is as much as we can stand.

We read the advertisements on the walls. We eye MR. SMITH'S bookstall till a small boy is told off to watch us, in the belief that we are there with a felonious intent.

We grow sulky, we get angry, we quarrel, we

make it up, and then it is time for ticket-taking. In exchange for something very like a five-pound note I get two tourists' return tickets for Saltington, and ROSE ANNA and I take our seats in a first-class carriage, and are soon whirling along the metals, away, far away, from smoky London to the clear fresh air of the sea and hills. Hurrah for Saltington !

It is a long hot fatiguing ride to Saltington. We sleep, I think, the latter part of the journey. At any rate, I jump up with a start when ROSE ANNA pinches my arm. I ask if it is a collision.

My wife says, enthusiastically, " No — THE SEA !"

Somebody else says, " The bright, the fresh, the ever free."

I look out of window and see about two inches of blue-grey vapour between a couple of hills. I wonder whether the sea at Saltington is always like that.

While I am wondering, the hills shut out even that little bit, and the train rushes on for Saltington.

" Tickets, gents ; tickets, please," says a voice.

" FULLALOVE !" roars another.

ROSE ANNA nudges me. I turn white and shiver.

" A gent of the name of FULLALOVE'S wanted," yells the same voice.

This is getting unpleasant. I put my head out of the carriage window and find everybody else has done the same, and that the majority are grinning.

I wait till the man comes close to me, when I ask, in a whisper, what he wants with MR. FULLA-LOVE. He declines to have any secrecy, but asks me, with the lungs of a Stentor, if *my* name is FULLALOVE.

I confess, tremblingly, that it is. Every eye in the train is directed towards me as he hands me a telegram. I open it with beating heart.

It is from COUTER AND PHLIMSY, and runs as follows :—

"Come back instantly. A mistake in your accounts. Return by next train."

ROSE ANNA says, " Don't go."

I think I'd better.

I inquire when the next train returns to town. I'm told if I sit where I am I shall be on my way back in a quarter of an hour.

I do sit, and am on my way back within the time mentioned. We reach London about two in the morning. I have no wish to prejudice people against ROSE ANNA, but I must say she was on the way, at all events, "grumpy."

Perhaps there was cause for it, too. Remember, we only saw two inches of sea!

I wish I knew what's wrong at COUTER AND PHLIMSY'S.

*　　*　　*　　*　　*

We deliberate, and decide to get home as fast as possible. We charter a cab at an exorbitant rate, and about three o'clock reach HIGHLOW Terrace.

MRS. MANTOWLER kindly offered to take charge of our house for us during our absence, so we know we shall be able to get in.

To our surprise we find our little home a blaze of light, while from an open window the sound of a harsh voice is borne to us on the morning breeze, announcing that the owner thereof considers himself a "chickaleary bloke."

What can this mean?

To come home the prey of anxiety, and with ruin staring one in the face, at three o'clock in the morning, to find one's house the abode of riot and debauchery! Distraction! as somebody says in some play.

We knock.

The servant after much delay, opens the door, and on seeing us thanks goodness with much fervour.

We ask the meaning of the lights, the music and the overpowering smell of tobacco.

She says Mr. Mantowler has arrived, and brought a few friends to spend a quiet even ing.

I inform Rose Anna that this is not to be borne, and am about to rush upstairs, when the servant detains me. She wants to know if she may speak to me.

There is something terribly mysterious in her manner. I follow her on tiptoe into the scullery

She says, " Hush !"

I hush.

She says in a thrilling whisper, " They've been after you."

I ask who ?

She says, I know.

I say I don't, and I ought to know best whether I know, though she declares she knows that I know.

(This sounds like a puzzle, but it's all right and will repay careful perusal.)

I insist on being told who has been after me.

She winks, and says, " The bailiffs."

I am knocked all of a heap by this announcement. I don't exactly know what a bailiff is like, but I fancy he must be the same sort of thing as a beefeater, and that I am about to be removed to durance vile on account of the unknown misdeed at COUTER AND PHLIMSY'S.

Seeing my horror and figurative prostration, the tongue of our mysterious servant is unloosed.

She continues, with marvellous rapidity, and without punctuation,—

"Yes sir and they got wind somehow or other about the place as you'd a-bolted leastways as you'd gone off without paying nobody and all the tradesfolk's been here a-cussin' and a-swearin' and a-leaving of their bills and the perlice has been about the dog-tax and the livery stable man he sent and said he'd thank you to settle that little matter of fifteen pun' and MR. COMPO he came sir and he said as how he'd have his money out in blood or furniture or something and please sir there's a quarter's wages due to me and please I'd like to have it and please I'd like to leave this day month."

This is the news that greets me on my return to HIGHLOW Terrace.

Upstairs I hear many voices declaring, "they always are so jolly, oh!" in a manner inducing me to believe that there can't be many full bottles left in my cheffonier.

I go upstairs, and have a notion of sneaking off
to bed without saying anything to anybody, leaving the riotous revellers in undisputed possession ;
but ROSE ANNA objects to such cowardly conduct, she says, and I enter the chamber of debauchery.

As soon as my manly form is recognized
through the tobacco-smoke, I am greeted with a
shout of welcome. Glasses of intoxicating beve-
rages are presented to me.

I drink to drown care. I am called upon for a
song. I commence the appropriate one of "The
Heart bowed down by Weight of Woe," but am
not allowed to conclude it. I am told I must
either sing something comic, or stand a champagne
breakfast.

I wonder who's the master of this house. I
don't exactly know what happens next, but I wake
on the floor, some hours afterwards, with a headache and the knowledge that I must go off at once
to COUTER AND PHLIMSY'S—in all probability to
hear that I am discharged—and that unless I can
obtain some money immediately to pay my cla-
morous creditors, I shall be doomed to pass the
remainder of my life in a gloomy dungeon in the
Tower, a permanently insolvent debtor.

At last the worst has come.

Upon reflection, however, I am not quite certain that it is the very worst. At any rate, things are in a bad way so far, and if there is worse coming I don't clearly see how I am to survive the suffering.

When I reach the office I see at a glance that there is something dreadfully wrong. On entering, I smile and nod to POPKINS. Instead of smiling and nodding back to me, POPKINS averts his gaze.

I say, "Good morning, MR. SIMPSON," to the head cashier ; but MR. SIMPSON makes no answer. It strikes me that the door-porter is uneasy when I speak to him, and that everybody, speaking generally, avoids my eye, and takes stock of me clandestinely from round a corner.

Presently PHLIMSY'S bell rings. The head cashier answers it, and, returning to the office, beckons me solemnly, after the fashion of the shade of the late lamented MR. BANQUO.

With a sort of giving-way-at-the-knee kind of feeling, I rise and follow him.

I find COUTER AND PHLIMSY drawn up in a line awaiting my arrival, and one of them says, "Look here, MR. FULLALOVE."

I assume that sprightliness which it is the custom of those low down in our house to assume when those who are high up speak to them.

MR. COUTER says, "We're very sorry, MR.

FULLALOVE, to have to make a serious complaint, but we are far from pleased with you."

Not exactly knowing what I ought to say under the circumstances, I say nothing. I am conscious of saying nothing, with my mouth very wide open and my eyes rolling. As MR. COUTER proceeds, my mouth opens wider and my eyes roll more.

MR. COUTER makes these remarks in continuation :—

"You are, in fact," says MR. COUTER, "utterly worthless and incompetent. You have never done half a day's work since you have been in the Bank. Your salary shall be paid to you to the end of the month, and you had then better go about your business."

Feeling that something in the shape of reply is absolutely imperative under these circumstances, I say, "Yes, sir."

MR. COUTER does not appear to think this answer altogether satisfactory, and goes on to add,—

"You are, I am afraid to say, MR. FULLA-LOVE, wholly and irreclaimably incorrigible. You have been intrusted with the care of the ledgers, sir. Look here, sir!—and here!—and here!"

He opens a fresh page at each "here," and points at certain portions with a trembling finger.

With a vague impression that there is some horrible mistake in the balances, I say,—

" Is it in the noughts, sir ?"

MR. COUTER, without heeding the remark, goes on excitedly turning over the pages.

" Twelve—fourteen—sixteen—twenty-two——"

" Twenty-two what, sir ?"

" Blots !" he says, in a voice of thunder, and wrenches at another leaf. The leaf he wants to open has, however, stuck fast to the next leaf, owing to a good deal of ink having been shut up between them accidentally, and, when parted, there is what is technically termed a black-beetle—a fine specimen.

MR. COUTER is enraged ; so is PHLIMSY. They say to one another, " Can we stand this ?" and decide they cannot. They decide, therefore, that I had better have my money and go. I take it, and presently make myself scarce.

On finding myself out in the open air, I am at first buoyant. Subsequently I despond a little. When I get home to HIGHLOW Terrace, I feel very low indeed, and tell ROSE ANNA that ruin stares us in the face.

She says, " O, bother !"

*   *   *   *   *

We have had words, ROSE ANNA and I, but

we are friends again. I have taken her to my bosom, and she is there at this moment. Later on we have tea, and talk things over.

On reflection ROSE ANNA writes to her mamma, who comes, bringing with her her papa, and we talk things over more lengthily.

It is ROSE ANNA'S mamma's opinion that I am a simpleton. ROSE ANNA'S papa is inclined to think that perhaps I am more of a noodle. At last they agree together that it shall be nincompoop. This decision is to be considered final.

*   *   *   *   *

Things have been very much talked over by this time, and ROSE ANNA and I are very miserable. It has been settled that we give up our house, and go into lodgings. When ROSE ANNA'S father can find some suitable employment, I am to have it ; but he don't seem certain as to what I am fit for.

ROSE ANNA and I vow eternal devotion, when we get the chance, for half a moment, out in the passage. Then she goes home with her mother. I am not quite clear where I am going, but I suppose it is all right; only I wish ROSE ANNA'S papa wouldn't interfere quite so much. If he does, we shall have some unpleasantness before long.

*   *   *   *   *

We have had unpleasantness. I have told him my house is my own, and he may go. I have written to ROSE ANNA, bidding her peremptorily to return.

*   *   *   *   *

ROSE ANNA'S papa is still here, and ROSE ANNA has not come. I am going to write again to ROSE ANNA.

*   *   *   *   *

I have written again. She sends back a long letter, crossed. She says she and her mamma have had a serious talk. She hardly thinks she and I are suited to each other. We had better part, it is her opinion. Perhaps we had.

On thinking things over, it seems to me this has been a very long honeymoon, or a very short one; or, perhaps, there has been no honeymoon at all, or if there has, it has been a honeymoon with no honey in it.

I wonder whether there are many other honeymoons without any honey in them? Many people who are "happy ever afterwards," and ever afterwards jolly miserable? Whether everything is a " ghastly mockery," a " hollow sham," and a " whitened sepulchre"?

Upon reflection, I have not the remotest notion.

T!:E END.

BILLING AND SONS, PRINTERS, GUILDFORD, SURREY.